WHAT'S A NICE HARVARD BOY ⸻ ⸻ ⸻
⸻ *LIKE YOU DOING IN THE BUSHES?*

WHAT'S A NICE HARVARD BOY LIKE

AN ASSOCIATED FEATURES BOOK ——

YOU DOING IN THE BUSHES?

by RICK WOLFF

Edited by Phil Pepe

Published by Prentice-Hall, Inc., Englewood Cliffs, N. J.

*This book is dedicated to the unknown minor leaguer
who, somewhere across this vast expanse of country known as
the United States, is probably reading this while
riding on yet another bus,
on his way
to play yet another ball game
tonight.*

What's a Nice Harvard Boy Like You Doing in the Bushes?
by Rick Wolff   Edited by Phil Pepe
Copyright © 1975 by Associated Features Inc.
Material reprinted from Popular Sports *Baseball* © 1974
CBS Publications is reprinted with the permission of
Popular Library Publishers.
Printed in the United States of America
Prentice-Hall International, Inc., London
Prentice-Hall of Australia, Pty. Ltd., Sydney
Prentice-Hall of Canada, Ltd., Toronto
Prentice-Hall of India Private Ltd., New Delhi
Prentice-Hall of Japan, Inc., Tokyo

10 9 8 7 6 5 4 3 2 1

Wolff, Rick.
    What's a nice Harvard boy like you doing in the bushes?

    "An Associated Features book."
    Autobiographical.
    1. Wolff, Rick.   2. Baseball.   I. Title.
GV865.W64A38   796.357'092'4   [B]   75-2499
ISBN 0-13-951814-2

ACKNOWLEDGMENTS

I have always considered that the achievement of professional status in sports is not due solely to the individual efforts of the athlete himself, but rather represents the composite result of the efforts of a multitude of people. I feel that my career is no exception. I would like, therefore, to acknowledge those who have coached, instructed, encouraged and helped me in becoming a "pro."

Mr. Art Mann, Mr. Eric Kantor and Mr. Karl Wiehe—for supplying me with a bedrock solid foundation of understanding sports, on which my career has always faithfully rested.

Mr. Al Goldis—for spotting a glimmer of potential in me as a pro ballplayer, and for devoting literally hundreds of hours in trying to mine that potential into a "big league" prospect.

Mr. Dom Napolitano, Mr. "Rabbit" Jacobson, and the late Mr. Emil Gall—for publicly recognizing this raw potential and giving me the opportunity to play pro ball for the Detroit Tigers (in the hopes of my being a "diamond in the rough").

Mr. Len Okrie—for taking this potential and working with it, trying to refine, sharpen and polish it into a true gem of Major League quality.

I'd also like to thank the members of my family—Mom, Dad, Bob and Marge—for their constant support throughout the good and especially through the lean seasons. Also, my thanks to Linda C. Coffin, M.D., who, although not a psychiatrist, helped me keep my perspective and sanity when the

0-for-4's began to pile up. Finally, my thanks to Vicki, Mary, Linda, Ellen, Nelson and other assorted members of the Harvard Class of '75 for their helpful comments and criticisms in the writing of this book.

Richard H. Wolff
Boston, Massachusetts

PREFACE

This book was born one night in Yankee Stadium, a most fitting birthplace.

I had known Rick Wolff and his family for, well, about half of Rick's life. I had watched him grow from boyhood, to young manhood, to manhood, a typical suburban youngster with typical interests.

Most of his spare time was taken up by sports. Rick tried them all, and excelled in most.

As best as I could, I followed his progress, as closely as the difference in our years and our interests would allow. I kept thinking of him as a football player, at Edgemont High in New York's Westchester County, then as a freshman halfback at Harvard.

I doubt if I saw him more than a dozen times over the past dozen years, one of those times being when I went to a game in the Atlantic Coast Baseball League, a local summer league made up of college players. Rick was playing second base that night. I don't even remember if he got a hit.

And then I heard he had been drafted by the Tigers and I ran into him in Tigertown during the spring of 1973, when I was covering the Yankees for the New York *News*.

Our next meeting was in Yankee Stadium in September, 1973. Rick was back from his first year of professional baseball at Anderson, South Carolina. We had dinner as he related his experiences as a rookie pro.

I was enthralled. He had experienced so much, and he told it so well. He was a natural storyteller with a wonderful sense of humor and sense of the absurd. He had a great ear for dialogue and a photographic memory for even the minutest detail.

I suggested a book. He agreed to put all his experiences of his first year at Anderson on paper, from memory, with the aid of scrapbooks and letters to his parents that they had saved.

When he was invited back by the Tigers for a second year, we decided to make the book a two-year diary and he kept notes on his 1974 experiences.

What follows is the result. Every word is Rick's. My contribution was subtraction, not addition; editing, not writing; for the original manuscript, if we let it run, would be twice as long as the finished product.

I am proud to have been a part of this book, happy to have had the ability to vicariously live Rick's two years in the minor leagues. But the reason I am most proud to have been a part of this book is because it gave me a better opportunity to know this exceptional young man.

Phil Pepe

As I was returning from my class on "The Psychoanalytic Aspects of the Law," I ran into a classmate whom I hadn't seen in months.

"I understand you're taking a leave of absence," he said.

"That's right," I replied. "I'm going off to play professional baseball for the Detroit Tigers."

My classmate looked at me, then broke into huge grin.

"That's a pretty good line, Rick," he blurted out. "But tell me, what are you REALLY going to do? Campaign down in Washington for a politician? Join the Peace Corps?"

"No, no," I answered. "I'm going to try to be a big league baseball player."

My friend cracked up with laughter.

"That's what I like about you," he said, "you're the only guy I know who can tell a joke with a straight face."

With that he walked off, cackling over the absurdity of someone taking a year off from Harvard to play a little boy's game.

As I continued to walk on, I ran into a former psychology professor of mine in the courtyard of my dormitory, Mather House. As we chatted, I mentioned that I was preparing to take a leave of absence. Naturally, he asked me what I was going to do.

"I'm going off to try my luck as a professional baseball player. You know, down in the minors."

His face scrunched up in confusion. "I'm not certain I

1

NELSON CHEN

What's a bush leaguer like me doing at Harvard?

Harvard's 1971 NCAA District 1 champs: I'm third from the right, top row.

understand. You say you're going off to the minors. What is that, something like summer stock?"

Rather than get involved in some long explanation that might be embarrassing, I simply nodded and said, "Yes, I guess you could say it's like I'm going into the performing arts."

The kindly old professor beamed with delight.

"Wonderful, Richard," he said. "You know, I had no idea that you possessed ability as an actor."

Neither did I, I thought.

With this, we departed, and as I resumed my walk back to the room, I began to ponder these curious little interactions. I guess I should have expected them. I mean, not too many Harvard students go off to play professional baseball. Most of my classmates will graduate and go on to study medicine or law or some other well-respected and traditional career.

With my decision, I may have set a precedent. I may have set Harvard tradition back 300 years.

En Route to Tigertown
February 22

I don't know if my nervousness is overshadowed by my excitement of going to my first spring training, but I'm on my way to a totally new experience, that of being a professional baseball player.

I vividly remember when the good news came. It was back in June of last year that I learned I had been selected in the free agent draft by the Detroit Tigers.

That initial moment of exhilaration practically numbed my senses. Then, when I grasped the impact of what had happened, I felt like exploding. I felt like running out of the house and into the street to shout to the world the incredible news. Imagine, after all the years of sweat and strain, of ups and downs, of successes and failures, to be chosen as one of the select few to play pro ball! It was simply a glorious, wonderful feeling.

4

ETROIT

roit, Michigan 48216 ◆ TELEPHONE 962-4000

June 7, 1972

. Richard H. Wolff
 Tanglewood Road
arsdale, New York

ar Rich:

    Congratulations! You have been selected
 the Detroit Organization in the Regular
ee Agent Draft. Our area scout will contact
u.

    With best wishes.

                              Cordially,

                              Ed. Katalinas

                              Edward G. Katalinas
                              Director of Scouting

K/gsk

My first reaction was pure elation, but then reason tempered my feelings. I had a big decision to make, the toughest decision of my life.

At first the Tigers wanted me to sign immediately and report to one of their rookie league teams for the remainder of the 1972 season. I resisted that, preferring to finish up my season in the Atlantic Collegiate Baseball League, a summer league in the New York–New Jersey area, and begin my professional career fresh in 1973.

That wasn't the big decision. I had one semester remaining to complete my studies as an undergraduate at Harvard and if I signed a professional baseball contract, I would have to leave school. It would mean postponing my graduation for a full year.

I was reluctant to lose that year, but anxious to try my luck at professional baseball. Anyone would be.

I had been drafted 709th out of 788 players and I realized that 709th draft choices are not treated like pheenoms; they are not expected to make it to the major leagues.

For weeks I wrestled with my decision, but eventually I decided to postpone my graduation, give up one semester and one year of my life to baseball. I just had to give it a shot. How else would I know if I could make it? I couldn't live with that unanswered question for the rest of my life.

It was with great pride that I signed my contract, the pride of knowing somebody thought I had some ability. Now, although the pride remains, the celebration is over. Now, on this plane, as I approach the beginning of my new pro career, my head is swimming with a thousand questions . . .

How should I prepare myself? What will it be like, living as a pro? Am I a good enough hitter to succeed? Are the fields in the minor leagues as bad as everybody says? Are the bus rides really that long? Am I in good enough physical shape? How many second basemen do the Tigers have in their organization? Am I good enough to make it to the big leagues?

This last question is one that is asked by anyone who has

ever picked up a bat or thrown a ball, of whom there must be millions. But, the fact remains that only a small number, a select minority of amateur players, will ever get the chance to play professional baseball. Only this small group will ever really get the chance to pursue the answer to that vital question. The rest can only dream.

And I guess, if nothing else, I now belong to that exclusive fraternity of professional athletes, and I will be fortunate enough to pursue that essential question. For this opportunity, whether I do or do not make it to the big leagues, I am, and always will be, grateful.

Oh, yes. It would be nice if I also got a few base hits along the way.

Lakeland, Fla.
February 23

I arrived at Tigertown, my home for the next two months, and practically the first thing that happened was that somebody handed me a booklet of six typewritten sheets with the heading: "TIGERTOWN RULES AND REGULATIONS."

As I flipped through the pages, I was struck by the thought that at Harvard, they take great pride in individual freedom. Nobody tells you how long you may wear your hair, whether or not you must attend classes and what time you must go to bed, or even if you must go to bed at all.

After the freedom of Harvard, Tigertown was going to be a drastic change of lifestyle. Here's what the instructions said:

"Welcome to Tigertown, John E. Fetzer Hall, and to the city of Lakeland. We are proud of our facilities at Tigertown and hope that each of you will enjoy them and use them to your advantage. We are pleased and privileged to house our personnel in John E. Fetzer Hall. We are certain you will enjoy its comforts.

"The following regulations and procedures have been prepared for your guidance. After reading them, we are expecting your complete cooperation and compliance since none of them are unreasonable in nature or intent.

"Please familiarize yourself with the contents of this bulletin and, if you are in doubt, ask someone for assistance.

GENERAL RULES

1. The following curfew and time schedule will prevail:
   a. Curfew is 11:30 P.M. with everyone in their respective rooms. Lights out at 12:00 midnight and all radios, televisions, stereos, etc. must be off. There will be periodic bed checks with automatic fines for missing bed check.
   b. The Snack Bar will close at 11:00 P.M.
   c. The First Floor Lounge will be closed to all visitors at 9:00 P.M. sharp. All other lounges are off limits to all except players and working personnel.
   d. 8:00 A.M. is wake-up call. Your room must be vacated by 9:30 A.M. to allow the maids to begin work.
2. Park in the designated places, watch your speed and be careful when driving in the area. There will be many persons concentrated in a small area so be alert when driving in the area. *The access road to Fetzer Hall is for deliveries only. Tell your friends!!*
3. Alcoholic beverages of any kind are not permitted in this training camp.
4. The use of, possession of, or sale of drugs of any kind, unless prescribed by a physician, is prohibited. The use of, possession of, or sale of marijuana is also prohibited. Such actions are illegal in the eyes of the Federal Laws of the United States and are felonies and misdemeanors depending on the circumstances. We are required to take appropriate action and will do so if a situation arises. You

8

face dismissal and loss of pay. The use of drugs is a serious problem confronting our young people. Don't be stupid!! Fail because of lack of ability not because you were unaware of your surroundings, obligations and responsibilities.

5. Gambling is not allowed in Tigertown and will not be tolerated during the season. Most of us cannot afford to gamble, friendships are lost, as well as proper rest, and it is not conducive to team play and team effort.

6. Minimum dress requirements:
   Bermuda shorts in the area and in the city are allowed. Shoes, not shower shoes, must be worn in the dining area. Cut-offs, football jerseys, T-shirts, and other sloppy attire are not in keeping with your profession. We expect all of you to keep yourself neat and properly groomed.

7. Watch your language in the dormitory, on the field, and in the cafeteria.

8. Each player will be entitled to a weekly laundry allowance of $2.50. Laundry will be picked up each Thursday morning and returned the following Tuesday. If your bundle exceeds your weekly allowance, you will be expected to pay the difference when you pick up your bundle. Details regarding this will be posted on Tigertown bulletin boards. Laundry bags and slips are available in the Snack Bar. Dry cleaning service is available at your expense.

9. Identification cards will be available to all players. They will be accepted as identification at the Florida National Bank in Lakeland if you desire to cash personal checks. They will, also, admit you free to Major League exhibition games at Marchant Stadium. You are not allowed in box seats nor is this card transferable. You must enter at the Pass Gate with this card. No checks will be cashed in the office or Snack Bar.

10. Transportation will be provided from Tigertown to down-

town Lakeland each evening and on Sunday mornings so that you may attend church services. This convenience will only be available so long as you conduct yourselves in a gentlemanly manner in town.

11. Hitchhiking to downtown Lakeland is permitted if done from the sidewalk. No hitchhiking permitted from the streets. This is a city ordinance and VIOLATORS WILL BE SUBJECT TO ARREST.

12. Tigertown offices are located on top floor of the Art Guild Building. *Stay out* unless you have something of importance to discuss with a club official. Discuss it with your manager first. In most cases, he will be able to help you. If he can't, we will be glad to see you.

13. Check bulletin boards frequently for work schedules, special information, and regulations. They are located on each floor of the dormitory and on the porch of the cafeteria.

14. Outgoing mail may be deposited and incoming mail may be picked up at the mail rack on the cafeteria porch. Players are not permitted to pick up mail in uniform during training breaks or during lunch period.

15. Station wagons used for road trips are obtained through the courtesy of automobile manufacturers in Detroit. We are responsible for maintaining them in good condition. No baseball shoes are to be worn in these wagons. Tailgates are to be closed at all times. Players are not to drive unless specifically assigned by a manager. No food or beverages allowed in wagons to prevent soiling of the upholstering.

16. Players must wear shirts when using the Recreation Room.

17. Treat recreation equipment as you would treat your own. There is a limit to the supply.
    No one will be permitted to use the pool tables or Ping-Pong tables during the breakfast or dinner hours.

Anyone caught abusing these tables will be prohibited from using them.

DORMITORY RULES

1. Each player will be assigned a specific room and any changes in these assignments will be made only with the approval of, and at the direction of, the camp director.
2. Each of you will be issued a room key. Lock your door whenever you leave and keep the key on your person at all times. DETROIT BASEBALL CLUB WILL NOT BE RESPONSIBLE FOR LOSSES OF ANY KIND DURING YOUR STAY IN TIGERTOWN. A SAFE IS AVAILABLE FOR VALUABLES AT THE AD-MINISTRATION OFFICE. USE IT.
3. Wives, children, parents and pets of any kind are not permitted in your room.
4. *Food of any kind as well as soft drinks of any kind may not be taken to your room.* The Snack Bar is available for your convenience. Please use the proper receptacles for disposing of all wastepaper and trash.
5. Do not hang any pictures, slogans, trophies, etc. on the walls or closet doors. Keep your rooms orderly and be considerate of others sharing your room. Our maids are required to notify the Camp Director of excessive dirt and any other violations of any type. Pick up all shoes, socks, etc. so our maids can clean properly.
6. Any damage to a room or its contents, or any missing fixtures will be paid for by the present occupants of that room. Inspections will be made regularly. *A room check and uniform check will be made before anyone receives transportation from Tigertown.*
7. The windows are sealed and cannot be opened, but we

11

DETROIT

I'm a Tiger in spring training.

shall try to keep the buildings at a comfortable temperature.

8. There will be no smoking in the rooms, but smoking is permissible in the lounges. Your cooperation and consideration of non-smokers will be appreciated.

9. Players in uniform are not allowed in Fetzer Hall at any time.

10. Shower shoes are compulsory when using the shower facilities in John Fetzer Hall.

CAFETERIA REGULATIONS

1. Meal schedule is as follows:

   BREAKFAST 8:30 A.M. to 9:00 A.M.   Mon.–Saturday
   9:00 A.M. to 10:30 A.M.   Sunday
   LUNCH   On the field (Check daily bulletins.)
   DINNER   5:30 P.M. to 6:30 P.M.   Mon.–Saturday
   4:30 P.M. to 5:30 P.M.   Sunday

   Fill up rear tables first. Do not loiter in the cafeteria after your meal.

2. Do not waste food and be sure you can eat all that you take. *Only one juice, salad, beverage, and dessert allowed to a player.* Within reason, and after all personnel have eaten, you may have as much of the main course as you want.

3. Minimum dress requirements prevail in the Cafeteria. They are: shoes or sandals, NOT SHOWER SHOES, Bermuda shorts or walking shorts, not CUT-OFFS, washable shirt, not a T-SHIRT and not a PULLOVER FOOTBALL SHIRT.

4. There is no need for profanity and abusive language. Those who are helping us in the Cafeteria are our most appreciated help and should be treated with consideration and respect. Any treatment to the contrary will invoke immediate disciplinary action.

5. Be certain to place your tray and empty dishes on the conveyor when you leave the Dining Room. Place your chair under the table.
6. COOPERATE.

CLUBHOUSE REGULATIONS & FIELD PROCEDURES

1. Check the Bulletin Board for late announcements.
2. Secure your wallet and valuables. We will not be responsible for any loss in the clubhouse.
3. Keep all shoes off the floor.
4. Hang your uniform properly after each day's use. We will not pick up after you.
5. Dispose of your sanitary socks in the proper receptacle.
6. No horseplay, whatsoever, in the clubhouse and showers.
7. Take your shower with consideration for those who follow. (Do not linger and replace soap.)
8. Whirlpool is to be used at the direction of the trainer. There is some danger attached if used improperly.
9. One towel is issued each day—please do not leave it on the floor. Place it in the basket after use.
10. Report all injuries to the trainer or if on the field, to your manager. It is not necessary for you to play when handicapped by any type injury. No player should visit any doctor without written permission from the trainer.
11. Do not grumble when your name is placed on another group. It is your job to get in proper shape and to learn as much as possible. It is our job to make final disposition of your contract.
12. No children, relatives, friends are allowed in the clubhouse. THE CLUBHOUSE AT MARCHANT STADIUM IS ABSOLUTELY OFF LIMITS TO ALL TIGERTOWN PLAYERS. DECLINE ANY SUCH INVITATIONS SINCE YOU WILL BE ASKED TO LEAVE.

13. Calisthenics and roll call must be taken before any daily activity begins.
14. All players should remain in the area for announcements regarding cancellation of work and the use of the hangar for workouts during any rainy or cold weather.
15. Lunch—on the porch—check your daily bulletins for any time changes. You may have one of each item. No seconds. Please throw your trash in the barrels provided. No lunch in the clubhouse unless verbally informed to do so by officials of Tigertown.
16. No extra workouts allowed unless approved and supervised. The use of the batting cage will, also, be supervised in all cases.
17. No player should leave his squad or the field without permission from his manager or coach.
18. Take care of the equipment provided and check your field before returning Tigertown equipment and bats.
19. Control your temper! Breaking, and throwing of bats, helmets, and equipment will result in disciplinary action and does your personal cause no good whatsoever. *Additionally, we will not tolerate any altering of outer socks which are provided for you. There will be an automatic $25.00 fine for altering outer socks and you will pay for a new pair.*
20. There will be no tailoring of baseball uniforms, in any way, without written permission of Mr. Evers.
21. Be careful of the sun. An extreme burn may harm your chances or set you back several days during this training period. The same caution should be exercised with blisters on hands and feet. Take care of them immediately and advise your manager and trainer of your condition. Wear old shoes at the beginning of training.

"At first glance, this may seem like far too many rules and regulations, but they have been listed to guide your actions. I am certain that most of you would conduct yourselves in such a manner without our having to list them in this bulletin.

In closing, the Detroit Baseball Club wishes each of you a successful Spring Training."

I wondered if they gave merit points to those who obeyed all the rules. Actually, I couldn't help thinking that, in the long run, base hits were going to be more important.

Lakeland, Fla.
February 24

Our first practice session ended about an hour ago, and now I'm back in my room at Fetzer Hall after a meal of franks and beans. I feel very much like a freshman in college again, surrounded by people, yet alone and totally isolated, far from my home and my friends, a little apprehensive, a little lonely, a little frightened.

My roommate is an eighteen-year-old shortstop from California named Bob Stevens. It's his first time away from home and I'm certain he feels lonelier than I do.

Our room has two beds, a small desk with a night lamp and a good view of the baseball fields about a hundred yards away. Beyond that is the major league complex, Marchant Stadium. The big leaguers live in the more plush Holiday Inn in downtown Lakeland.

Our first practice session was an experience in itself. About 170 guys filed into this little wooden clubhouse, the minor leaguers' dressing room. It is old and small, filled to capacity with wooden and wire cubicles, row after row. Everybody, each prospective big leaguer, is issued a nice doubleknit uniform with a big, fancy old English "D" over the left breast and a cap with a patched-on "D" on it. Unfortunately, due to the large amount of ballplayers, all the uniforms come with football numbers. I'm your typical second baseman, number 89.

16

The veterans talk about old times, but the rookies, like me, meander around aimlessly, trying to give the impression we know what we're doing.

Finally, Ed Katalinas, a kindly bear of a man who's the Director of Scouting, roars in a deep, husky voice over a PA that everyone should run out for calisthenics. After calisthenics, we warmed up, took a little batting practice in which we all tried too hard and almost nobody hit well, packed it in and went back to shower.

Back in the dorm, everybody walks around sizing everybody else up. It's a rather uncomfortable feeling, but one has to realize that everyone wants to survive through spring training and get a job for the summer. As for me—well, I haven't done anything wrong yet.

Lakeland, Fla.
March 1

I'm beginning to get a feel for this place. Everybody seems to have his place in the hierarchy of the Detroit organization. For example, a quick stroll through the minor leaguers' parking lot will reveal exactly where one stands on the social ladder. The big bonus babies have brand-new cars, with all the trimmings. Some even have license plates with their initials on them.

Then come the foreign sports cars, which belong to the guys who got big money but not enough to afford a big, snazzy car.

Finally, there are the bombs that seem ready to fall apart, but are at least utilitarian if not graceful. They form the great bulk of cars here, the base of the social structure.

The reason I mention the cars is that a ride in an automobile to a laundromat in Lakeland is a big night out. The laundromat is in downtown Lakeland, about two miles from Tigertown. In order to get there, everybody piles into a car and we take off. At the laundromat, while the clothes are washing, one can saunter through the streets of town. To-morrow we may even browse in the comforts of the Lakeland Mall, a shopping area. I can hardly wait.

"Hey, let's throw!"

The big voice boomed down at me and as I turned around and looked up, and up, I saw the immense, unmistakable form of Big Frank Howard. And I mean big. He kept rising up in the air, I thought he'd never stop. I guess I must have been staring with my mouth and eyes wide open because he said it again.

"Let's throw a little."

I nodded and, trying to be as casual as I could, I began throwing with him. Imagine, Frank Howard asking me to catch with him!

There had been an exhibition game scheduled against the Montreal Expos today and most of the Expos' big league team was playing. Detroit sent over several big guys, like Frank Howard, Ike Brown and Tony Taylor, but most of the team was made up of the top AAA players in the organization. To give us a thrill, they let some of us rookies make the trip. And here I was, having a catch with Frank Howard in front of the Tiger dugout.

I didn't know whether to thank him for his graciousness in honoring me or to try to appear casual, as though I always warm up with big leaguers. For that matter, I didn't even know how to address him. Do I call him Frank? Mr. Howard? Hondo? I guess he must have realized my nervousness because he just started throwing to me.

After a while, he stopped and came over to me. He began asking me to point out all the rookies and tell him their names.

I didn't understand the purpose of this interrogation until the game started. While sitting on the bench, he was unbelievable. Big Frank Howard was actually leading the cheers, calling the rookies by their first names, and shouting encouragement at them in complete sincerity. Do you know what it's like to have Frank Howard yell and cheer for you, calling you by your name as though you're old buddies?

As the game proceeded, I was sitting on the bench, just happy to be there. The Tigers had tied the game in the ninth and we were going into extra innings. In the top of the eleventh, Johnny Lipon, who was managing the team, shouted at me to get loose and to go in and play second base.

I almost swallowed my chewing gum. I mean only Billy Martin, General Manager Jim Campbell and Hoot Evers, the Director of Player Development, were watching the game. I felt like a George Plimpton caricature. But there I was on the field, taking a few practice ground balls at second. The Expo leadoff batter, Larry Lintz, walked and on the next pitch, he broke for second. Instinctively, I dashed for the bag. I arrived there only to see the ball tailing off, right into the path of the base runner. A collision was inevitable. Yet, somehow, I caught the ball and while tumbling to the ground with the runner, I held onto it. Lintz was out and I was an instant star.

As I came back to the bench, I was congratulated by all the Tigers. The next thing I knew, it was the last of the thirteenth and I was in the on-deck circle, watching the batter ahead of me walk. Now I was at bat and my job was to bunt him over. Again my nervousness surfaced. I looked out at Balor Moore, the Expo pitcher, and he didn't seem terribly upset by the prospect of my hitting prowess. I didn't see the first pitch. But the catcher and the umpire did. Strike one. On the second pitch, I feebly attempted a bunt and it dribbled foul down the first-base line. Two strikes. The bunt was off. This was my chance to be a hero, to impress the brass with my hitting. I swung and the ball trickled down to the first baseman,

19

who forced the runner at second. I was on first base, the winning run.

The next batter, Hal Underwood, singled to center, advancing me to second. It was first and second, one out, and Frank Howard coming to bat. Now I'm the key runner. If I score, it's all over. If Howard hits a line shot somewhere, it's up to me to leg it home. But these are major league arms in the outfield. I decided to get a bigger lead off second.

While I was edging off, thinking about rounding third with the winning run, Moore wheeled around and threw to Lintz, the second baseman, who held the ball in his glove and had this big, pie-eating smile on his face. Panic-stricken, I bolted toward third. Lintz's throw hit me squarely in the back and I was safe and Underwood moved to second.

I was feeling pretty good about this nifty maneuver until I realized the Expos were giving Howard an intentional walk to load the bases. My blunder had taken the bat out of Frank Howard's hands. With the bases loaded, another rookie promptly grounded into a double play to end the inning.

The Expos scored a run in the fourteenth and we were beaten. I had denied Frank Howard a chance to drive in the winning run. I might be going home sooner than I thought.

Lakeland, Fla.
March 14

Ed Katalinas called my name over the loudspeaker during the morning practice and the sound of my name made my heart jump. Was I being released already?

I trotted over to Ed, trying not to betray my fear. He explained that a commercial was being filmed that afternoon over on another field and they needed a ballplayer to stand in. He asked if I would mind. Of course, I gleefully accepted.

When the trucks had unloaded all of their equipment including cameras, reflectors, monitors, and so on, I figured it was about time to report. Unfortunately, I didn't know who to report to and a crowd had begun to mill around the area. Bill Freehan, decked out in a Detroit uniform, was approaching the area, followed by a flock of autograph seekers.

Undaunted, I strolled over to one of the cameramen and asked for the director. I introduced myself as "the man they wanted from Tigertown," and the director quickly explained my role.

The whole thing didn't last more than twenty minutes, because Freehan was articulate with the commercial lines. It was an Air Force recruitment commercial. I was supposed to be batting in a game, check my swing at a pitch, then watch as Freehan argued with the umpire. Freehan then went into a transition from baseball to the Air Force and that was it.

When it was finished, the director handed me $50. I began to think maybe I was in the wrong business. Should I stay here and become the next Al Kaline or go to Hollywood and become the next Robert Redford? Decisions, decisions.

Lakeland, Fla.
March 22

Stubby Overmire, one of the minor league managers, came over to me and told me I'd be playing at Anderson, South Carolina, this year. It wasn't official yet, but it was the first encouraging word I had.

He also told me that my shortstop partner would be Hal Underwood and I immediately looked Hal up and suggested we work together on double plays.

Hal is a skinny black kid from Detroit, about six feet and 160 pounds, who has been in the Tiger organization a few years. He has thin legs and thin arms, but he has very graceful, fluid moves. He looked like he was going to be a good double-play partner.

It became official today. Assignments were posted on the bulletin board. I'll be playing for Anderson in the Class A Western Carolinas League. My manager will be Len Okrie, who played in the big leagues for four seasons with Washington and Boston.

I remembered the first time I met him. My dad had known Len slightly in Washington, where Dad was a radio broadcaster, so I decided to introduce myself to Okrie this spring.

"Len," I said, "I'm Rick Wolff. You knew my dad in Washington."

"So you're Roger Wolff's boy," he said.

Roger Wolff was a pitcher for the Senators, one of five knuckleballers on the Senators' staff, and Okrie was a catcher. As nicely as I could, I told Len that my dad's name is Bob, not Roger.

Here I am, deep in the heart of Dixie, right smack in the middle of true, blue, red-blooded Americana—Minor League Baseball.

It all started this morning at the ungodly hour of 5:30 when the guys assigned to Anderson assembled, bags packed, in the lobby of Fetzer Hall. Dave Miller, the Assistant Director of Player Development, put me in charge of the entourage and we boarded a chartered bus for Tampa to catch a 7:00 A.M. flight to Atlanta.

When we finally got to Atlanta we had a one-hour layover before continuing to Anderson on a Southern Airways flight. The plane was an old DC-3, with musty, dusty seats and worn carpeting. The flight was brutal.

Like a Hoyt Wilhelm knuckleball, we bounced up and down, dipped and dived, rattled and rolled over the muddy red rivers of Georgia and the country that was used in the filming of the movie *Deliverance*. I looked at Jack Walsh sitting next to me. His stomach was obviously taking a beating from the ride, so I started to inch away from him, expecting the worst.

Then I looked across the aisle at Santiago Garcia, a big, friendly kid from the Dominican Republic with a perpetual white smile on his dark face. He, too, was suffering, the smile had disappeared and he seemed to be mumbling something in Spanish, no doubt praying.

I felt he was ready to go at any time, and so rather than be caught in a double cross-fire trap like Scylla and Charybdis, I decided to get up.

At that moment, I spied the stewardess coming down the aisle with a supply of air sickness bags. She didn't look too well, either. I stopped her, mercifully looked up at her and asked her how far it was to Anderson. She pondered the question for an instant, took on a puzzled look and admitted she didn't know.

After about an hour of this prolonged torture, the same stewardess came on the PA and announced we were approaching Anderson, Georgia. That perked us up because we thought we were headed for some lost place called Anderson, South Carolina.

No sooner had this uneasy thought alarmed us than we landed. I glanced out the window to see what this place was like. A sign, handwritten, had scrawled on it, "Anderson, S.C." We had arrived. I looked out again at a school which was right next to the airport; the teacher had apparently brought the classes out to see an airplane. Instinctively, something told me this was going to be a small town.

We were greeted by a warm South Carolina sun and hospitality. Waiting for us was the team's general manager, bus

23

WILFRID

The Tiger greeting us on our arrival in Anderson
is team representative Bobbie Montgomery, and
that's shortstop Hal Underwood.

driver and bus owner, Bobby Kerr. The other member of the greeting committee was attired in a Tiger costume. It turned out to be the club secretary, Bobbie Montgomery.

It was obvious that I was a long way from Cambridge. What's more, I didn't think there was a Harvard club in the area.

We had a practice session and a team meeting this evening and I got my first look at my new working quarters—the Anderson County Memorial Stadium.

Located in an idyllic spot between the town cemetery and the county garbage dump, the ballpark consists of a large, uncovered grandstand extending from the third base line around the backstop and up the first base line. It has orange and blue plank boards for the spectators' seats and behind the grandstand is a two-story cinder block construction with the office upstairs and the refreshment stand below.

The outfield is vintage minor league, the fence splattered with an assortment of advertisements for local businesses. In left field, a giant lighted scoreboard, mounted on Pepsi-Cola and Seven-Up signs, keeps the vital information during games.

The infield looked beautiful from the stands, but closer inspection revealed a geologist's dream world of rocks, stones and pebbles. During infield practice, my worst fears materialized—the infield was as hard as cement and with all the rocks on it, it seemed certain my chest, arms and fielding average were all going to take a beating this season.

We assembled down in the clubhouse, another cinder block construction right next to the town dump. My ever sensitive olfactory nerves sensed very quickly that if the wind wasn't blowing in the right direction, the ballpark would be enshrouded in an unusual fragrance of old burnt tires and rotten vegetables.

Anderson County Memorial Stadium—there's
no place like home.

The clubhouse is just what I thought it would be like, small and cramped and filled with temporary wooden lockers. The wooden beams are covered with the names of former Anderson players scribbled in black magic marker. Spider webs are plentiful in the clubhouse and the cement floor is a lovely checkered pattern of tobacco juice and squashed bugs.

Our uniforms, however, are truly big league—brand new doubleknits with "Tigers" in script on the chest, with blue and orange trim. There's always something indescribably magical about putting on a new uniform.

Before we went on to the field, our manager, Len Okrie, held a brief meeting, telling us what he expected from us in the way of dress, hustle, and so on.

Len is an extremely tall man, about six feet five. At a quick glance, he bears a facial resemblance to Karl Malden, the actor.

Len is in his fifties and you can tell he has been through many, many minor league seasons. One thing that impresses you about him immediately is that he has incredibly straight, perfect posture. I have never seen him sloping down with his shoulders bent at an awkward angle. He walks with perfect posture and carries himself with a great deal of pride.

When you shake hands with Len, the first thing you notice is the size of his hands. He was a catcher and his hands are enormous. Your hand gets buried in his. It just seems to engulf yours like a huge bear paw.

His knuckles are scarred and battered from foul tips, and shaking hands with him, like Joe Garagiola says, is like sticking your hand in a bag of peanuts.

He seems to be in good shape, tall and lean with light brown hair that is barely getting gray.

He chews tobacco and speaks in a slight southern drawl and with a nice, soft, fatherly approach.

"We got a good little ball club here," he told us. "If we all work together . . . don't eat that popcorn and peanut crap before the game . . . that stuff ain't good for ya . . . Look out

27

for the girls, they're just waitin' to latch on to a prospect. No jeans on the road. All you guys can afford good, presentable clothes. We all got to work together, for there's plenty of room to advance in this organization."

Oke went on for about twenty minutes, telling us what's expected of us, then we went out and he pitched batting practice and hit infield practice, then told us to find ourselves a place to stay and settle down.

The season was opening in two nights. The Western Carolinas League was a Class A league with six teams including Anderson. Five of the teams were in South Carolina, the other, Gastonia, was in North Carolina, two hours away by bus.

We would be traveling exclusively by bus, to Greenwood, which was a half-hour ride; to Spartanburg, an hour and a half; to Gastonia, two hours; to Orangeburg, three and a half hours; and—the longest trip—to Charleston, a four-and-one-half-hour journey.

It wasn't a happy prospect traveling four and a half hours on a bus in Carolina heat. Not only that, the field was filled with rocks, the clubhouse filled with bugs and the smells from the dump would get to be unbearable.

All of these things might have made the summer ahead a dismal thing to look forward to, but somehow, with my first professional game just forty-eight hours away, I was filled with anticipation and exhilaration.

Anderson, S.C.
April 12

After searching frantically for a place to stay, four of us found a second-floor flat in a nice residential home.

My roommates are Jack Walsh, a pitcher with a strong New York accent and background; Steve Tissot, a pitcher who is also a guitarist and philosopher; and Fern Poirier, an outfielder from Montreal who speaks French better than he does English and with whom I am looking forward to conversing in his native tongue and polishing up my French.

Down below us is an elderly couple, the Taylors, who don't say much but always seem to be listening. Whenever they think we're a little too rowdy, they come up the stairs with an armful of fresh towels and linen and look around. Needless to say, in our first two days here we've accumulated quite a collection of towels.

Our place is slightly cramped. We have two bedrooms, one with three beds and the other with a double bed, a small kitchen and living room, also a tiny bath without a shower, just a bathtub. It's cozy, but for $50 a month each, we couldn't expect the Executive Suite.

Anderson, S.C.
April 13

Tonight was opening night in the Western Carolinas League. I didn't get to play in the first game, my first disappointment in Anderson. Without me, the team lost to Greenwood, which should tell them something.

I thought about going in to see Okrie and telling him, "Play me or trade me," but I decided to wait a few more days before making any ultimatums.

Greenwood, S.C.
April 14

This was our second game, a home-and-home series with the Greenwood Braves. I started at second base, batting eighth. On my first professional at-bat, in a typically dramatic fashion (how else?) I got a hit.

Let the historians note that it was not a bunt or a puny single, but a line drive triple to right center, one hop off the

ANDERSON
TIGERS
THE TEAM TO SEE IN 73

1973 SOUVENIR SCOREBOOK

25¢

1973
SCOREBOOK

Fast-Fun-Exciting-Live Action

wall. I was so excited that when I slid into third, I almost missed the bag. In my other three times, I walked twice and flied out to right.

In the field, I had a couple of tough chances and handled them all, and I even turned a double play. The game was super exciting, the lead changing hands until we put across the winning run in the ninth. Steve Litras drove in Ben Hunt with a single and we won, 5–4, our first victory of the year.

I'm an undefeated second baseman, fielding 1.000, batting .500 and, no doubt, leading the league in triples. I guess I'll be moving up soon to take Dick McAuliffe's job in Detroit.

Today, I learned firsthand about one of the joys of minor league baseball, the long bus ride.

We were forewarned in spring training that the minor league ballplayer's equipment includes bat, glove, spikes and a seat on the bus, not necessarily in order of importance, but it wasn't until today that I fully became aware of what a bus ride really meant.

Actually, I'm lucky, for the Western Carolinas is relatively compact, the bus rides not very long. The trip to Charleston is the longest, four hours.

We really have a nice bus, as buses (or is it busses?) go. I mean if you're queer for buses, you can freak out over this one, a double-decker, air-conditioned beauty. It belongs to Bobby Kerr, our GM and bus driver *de luxe*.

Bobby is quite a character. A small, wiry guy with an authentic southern drawl, Bobby is a genuine entrepreneur. He owns the ball team, three gas stations in Anderson, the bus which he rents out, and other assorted ventures. A flashy dresser, Bobby greases his hair straight back and that makes him look like he stepped right out of the 1950s. He can be

31

seen cruising around town in a fire-engine-red Cadillac and sporting a wallet full of $100 bills.

But Bobby's real passion is race-car driving and he uses the long bus rides to act out his fantasies. He fancies himself as the next Mario Andretti or A. J. Foyt and he cruises along the back roads of South Carolina at speeds up to 85 miles an hour.

Not surprisingly, as the season progresses, the seats in the back of the bus will become increasingly popular. Everybody figures when (not if, but when) we hit a tree or a truck, those in the back would have the best chance for survival.

Gastonia, N.C.
April 23

This was our first visit to Gastonia, a two-and-a-half-hour bus ride from Anderson.

When I first heard of Gastonia, the name intrigued me. I had visions of Groucho Marx raising his eyebrows, twirling his cigar and welcoming us to his land of plenty.

At the ballpark, the visitors' locker room is located right next to the public john. That's really not so bad, the sound of flushing water relaxes me before a game, but all of my puffed-up, vainglorious dreams of being a pro ballplayer lost a little steam when I signed an autograph for a fan who was simultaneously balancing a beer with one hand and zipping up his fly with the other.

When I moved on to the playing field, my initial impression came, of all places, from my feet. I looked down just in time to see my freshly polished spikes sink into a quagmire of soggy sand. Steve Litras, who had just made the same discovery of the field's terrain, yelled at me, "Hey, Wolffie, this infield reminds me of Jones Beach at high tide."

It is painfully obvious that the baseball term "grass cutter" is not part of the Gastonian lingo.

32

The fans sit up in wooden seats behind home plate, protected by a wire mesh screen that prevents foul balls from hitting them. From another perspective, that same wire mesh protected us, the visiting team, from the fans. Unfortunately, the screen wasn't soundproof as well. We were shielded from physical abuse, but still exposed to a verbal barrage.

They decided early in the game that they would pick on Bob Wisniewski, our tall and lanky catcher. Then they switched to Brian Sheekey when Sheek came in to pitch relief.

Sheek is from New Jersey and a graduate of the University of Rhode Island, where he worked on the university radio station as a disc jockey. He's a cocky guy with big city sophistication, an operator who always gets the upper hand. He's not the type to be ruffled by a crowd, but this one seemed to get to him.

At the end of one inning, he came running off the mound (and it's rare that the Sheek runs anywhere) and hid in the safety of the dugout.

"Man," said the Sheek, "this crowd must be the cast rejects from *The Waltons.*"

Anderson, S.C.
April 28

Let the record show that I, Rick Wolff, hit the Anderson Tigers' first home run of the 1973 season. I got a high fast ball, swung the bat and, presto, the ball just jumped over the Wometco Vending Company sign in left-center field, about 390 feet away.

I can't tell you what a feeling it was to circle the bases nonchalantly as though it happens all the time, and all the while trying to suppress a gigantic grin.

A truly tremendous experience. I must do it again sometime.

33

WILFRID BINE

The one, the only, the unforgettable Brian
(The Sheek) Sheekey.

I got my first glimpse of the famous Jimmy Piersall, the Orangeburg manager.

Orangeburg has an old ballpark, a throwback to old-time minor league baseball. The stands are made of weathered wooden planks and covered by a porous wooden roof. The field is enclosed by a cement wall, complete with the usual advertisements of local businesses. Beyond the outfield wall are the railroad tracks, which are fairly busy and incredibly noisy and dirty.

All of the guys on our team were anxious to see Piersall, the man and the legend, and of course the fans pay their money to see him climb a screen or something.

He didn't disappoint us. When he came out to home plate for the usual pre-game ritual of presenting his lineup card to the umpires, he didn't casually stroll out as most managers do. Instead, he burst out of the dugout, sprinted toward home and executed a perfect bent-leg slide into the plate.

Anderson, S.C.
April 30

Pay day. My pay is $500 a month, about average for a rookie. Out of that, over $125 is taken out in taxes. About $50 a month goes for food, $50 a month for rent, $100 a month for miscellaneous stuff like clothing, phone bills, laundry.

That leaves $175 a month. Oh, yes, on the road, we get $5 a day for meals.

I figure if I'm frugal, if I don't get too extravagant about luxury items like beer, I will have netted the staggering sum of $875 from my baseball efforts this summer, not including the $50 from the Freehan commercial.

I thought professional athletes made wads of money, drove big cars and wore fancy clothes. Who do I see about correcting this discrepancy?

Former Red Sox star Jimmy Piersall, manager of the Orangeburg Cardinals, was a show in himself.

Several weeks at the Taylors' residence was about all I could take. It was too cramped and as the warm weather started to come in, I realized I couldn't make it through the summer without an air conditioner. So I started looking around for another place.

I heard that George Cappuzzello, a young left-handed pitcher on the team, was looking for a new roomie. He had found a two-bedroom trailer and wanted someone to share the expenses. I decided to give it a try and after some negotiations with Cappy, started packing up to move to the trailer.

The trailer camp, "Green Acres," is located on the outskirts of town and right from the start I could see this was going to be a totally new concept in community living.

I discovered that, in a rectangular trailer, one can't make any right or left turns. All one can do is walk forward or backward. My bedroom is air-conditioned, but the rest of the trailer isn't, so that on really hot days the metal trailer performs like aluminum foil, roasting Cappy and myself like two baked potatoes.

Occasionally, we open the curtains in the living room and look out onto our neighbor's trailer, about 40 feet away. We have an exquisite, breathtaking view of the neighbor's garbage cans, his two half-starved monstrous dogs and his clothesline, which is always cluttered with underwear and blue overalls.

I always relax after a tough day by gazing out at this peaceful scene, this quaint bit of Americana. I must confess, though, that I observe this lovely setting only until the two gigantic mongrels notice me and visibly start to salivate at the prospect of making one of my limbs their dinner. At that point, I'll close the curtains and lock the door to the trailer.

Of course, like our clubhouse, the trailer is a veritable gold mine for any entomologist, for we have all sorts of insects living with us. A few days ago I noticed a small but steady stream of ants on a safari in my bedroom. The thick plush carpet makes a great cover for them and their jungle-like activities.

The other night, Cappy and I battled a determined wasp until 2:00 A.M. in our kitchen. Cappy, who is just as chicken as I am about stinging insects, was of little help as we finally prevailed in our microcosmic *Hellstrom Chronicle.*

Today, I went to hang up the wash on our clothesline and encountered a new breed of flying pests. Big and shiny green, about the size of a ripe grape, these beetles fly around all over the place and are particularly curious about new things, like me, for example. I have dubbed them "buzz bombers," for they come swooping down and use my arms as a runway. Although they're probably harmless, I don't give them a chance to test their arsenal. I give them a quick brush-off and flee back to the trailer for safety.

But the trailer and the bug population are not as exciting as some of the Homo sapiens who share this peaceful vista with us.

My first contact with the other residents was innocent enough, or so I thought. A little kid came to our door and asked if we wanted our lawn cut. I looked out on the small patch of barren red clay which resembled the surface of the moon and kindly declined his offer.

The kid looked up at me and cursed me out with a salvo of obscenities that would have been shocking if I heard them in our clubhouse.

The next day I happened to look out the window and saw my young friend running around the neighborhood playing cops and robbers. He was carrying a real shotgun. That might lower my sales resistance if he calls again.

Last night, though, was something else. Around midnight, one of the couples down the road had some sort of marital spat. It was a classic knock-down, drag-out battle with plenty of sound effects. We got to the door just in time to see the man of the family go crashing through the glass living-room window. Then the wife flung open the front door and started throwing bottles and plates after him, all the while unleashing a torrent of expletives.

By now, the man had jumped into his car, revved it up and started to drive toward the woman who was perched on the steps that lead to the front door. She barely escaped inside as the car smashed into the trailer, shattering more windows and destroying most of the front half of the trailer.

It was quite a show, but not unusual. The same couple goes through pretty much the same routine every weekend. Apparently, they spend the rest of the week patching up their feelings and the trailer, too.

Anderson, S.C.
May 3

The first statistics of the year were printed in today's paper. I would hardly consider it recommended reading. According to our official scorer, guardian and master of my fate, I'm cruising along with a potent .250 batting average—not too bad, but definitely not All-Star material.

I got to thinking, which I understand is a fatal process for potential big leaguers, about the role of the .250 hitter in American folklore.

There is something in our heritage about being a .250 hitter. It's hard to define, but without question, the .250 hitter is the backbone of our society. Statistically, .250 means one is averaging a hit out of every four attempts, but the allegorical symbolism of being a .250 hitter is something to be snickered at, not praised.

By contrast, a .300 hitter is a marvel, a demagogue, a true up-and-coming star whose life is golden and glorious. The guy who hits .300 has attained greatness in his lifetime and is held up to the masses as the ideal.

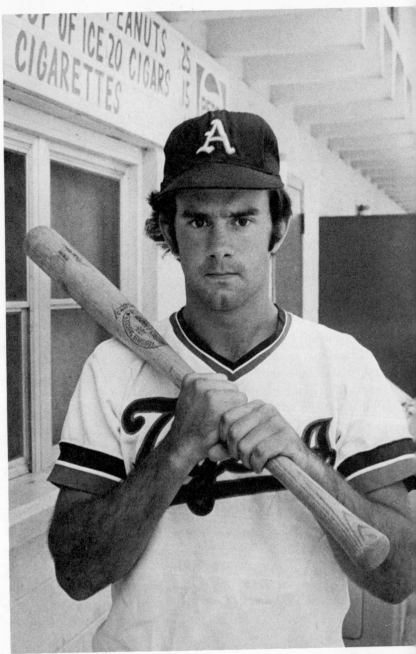

ANDERSON DAILY

I hope my favorite Louisville Slugger doesn't
have too many holes in it.

At the other end of the spectrum is the .200, or lower, hitter. Very little is written about these unfortunate wretches, for certainly their lives have been predestined by forces beyond our control. They exhibit little ability to hit the simple fast ball, much less a sharp curve. They are to be pitied, but not scorned.

But the .250 hitter remains an enigma, and enigmas always bother people. The .250 hitter has touched greatness on occasion (a three-for-four day or a game-winning hit), but he has also fallen just as often into the dark miserable abyss of going hitless, striking out with the bases loaded. A batting average of .250 is a trap, a limbo where few survive and fewer retain their sanity. It is a hellish experience, a nightmare come to life, Dante's Inferno.

It all came to a head last night when I grounded to shortstop. Since I was the third out of the inning, I tossed my batting helmet to Steve Tissot, the ol' philosopher, who had been coaching first base.

Naturally upset by making an out, I cursed my luck. Tis, overhearing me, walked by and shot me a knowing glance.

"Imagine, Rick," he said, "going through your entire life as just a .250 hitter."

Gastonia, N.C.
May 4

"Look out, everybody, Hoot's coming to town!"

The news came last week when Len gathered the guys together and told us not to panic or be uptight when Hoot came. But his efforts were futile. Instant panic besieged the team.

Hoot, you see, is Walter A. (Hoot) Evers, a pretty good outfielder for the Tigers in his day and now the club's Director of Player Development.

Hoot is the boss. He decides who gets released and who

41

gets promoted and in his hands is our fate. To insiders, Hoot is recognized as the "Masterful Magician of the Minor Leagues," for with one swift stroke of his pen, he can sign your unconditional release and instantly transform a professional ballplayer back into a common, ordinary civilian. He wields tremendous power and all ballplayers are mindful of his words. So when he comes to visit during the season, everybody starts to bear down just a little harder.

I have met the man only a few times. I'll never forget the first time, back in spring training. I had just played what I thought was a particularly good game, but I was taken out in the sixth inning after I was hit in the back of the head by an errant relay throw while I was sliding into third base. After the game, my head hurt, but I was feeling pretty good about my performance until Hoot came up behind me and barked, "Did you hurt your leg with that horseshit slide into third? That had to be the worst slide I've ever seen!"

I was stunned. I just mumbled something incoherent, trying in vain to apologize to Hoot and explain at the same time. My mumblings seemed to irritate Hoot even more. But before he could start on a new tirade, Jack Tighe, a nice man who is a Tiger super scout, came up and rescued me by explaining to Hoot that I had been hit in the head.

Hoot, obviously not too satisfied with this explanation, just cursed again and stalked off in search of new prey.

My fear of Hoot was shared by the entire team and so when he finally arrived all the guys pushed hard to impress him with their individual talents. Unfortunately, with all the pressure of trying to do well, everybody started to screw up.

We had to play Gastonia, which was going to be tough enough without Hoot there. With him there, it was going to be worse. We all got on the bus, but nobody uttered a sound, not even the usually vociferous Sheek.

After the two-hour ride, we pulled into the Howard Johnson's restaurant for dinner, as usual. But as Hoot and

Oke started to enter, the manager of the restaurant closed the door in their faces. He explained that the last time the Anderson baseball team was there, a couple of the guys had skipped out without paying their checks. That made a very nice impression on Hoot, but it only foreshadowed other disasters.

From that point on, everything went wrong. The harder we tried to impress Hoot, the more we fouled things up. I was a case in point. I decided to show Hoot how brilliant a base runner I was, so the first time I reached first base, I planned to steal second. With a right-handed pitcher and an erratic catcher, I figured I was a cinch. Needless to say, the ball was waiting for me at second base when I arrived.

That was embarrassing and as I glanced up at Hoot in the stands, I could see him scribbling something in his little notebook, probably about my speed.

I was so upset that when the chance repeated itself later in the game, I just had to vindicate myself. I mean, here was a pitcher who was so wild that you had to point him in the direction of home plate. And at the other end was a catcher who couldn't even throw out the garbage. I raced to second again. Again I was out by a mile.

My act of being thrown out twice in one game was eclipsed somewhat by Hal Underwood, a surefire base-stealer. He got picked off twice. Other guys misplayed singles into doubles, lost fly balls in the sun during night games, made bad throws.

I got the feeling Hoot was going to be waving his magic pen around quite a bit in the near future.

Anderson, S.C.
May 5

A funny incident occurred on my third at-bat against Spartanburg. I hit a drive off the left-center field wall that just missed going out by a few feet. Instead the ball bounced off the Navy

43

Recruiting sign and I had to settle for a double. That wasn't the funny part. I hit doubles all the time.

What was funny was that it happened during a typical minor league promotion gimmick called "Home Run for the Money." The way it works is a lucky ticket holder gets a cash prize if the designated hitter for him hits a home run in the prescribed inning.

Just before I came to bat in the seventh, the PA announcer said this was the "Lucky Home Run for the Money" inning and that if I hit one out, the ticket holder would win $70. The guy who held the lucky ticket was a fan with a great pair of leather lungs and just as I was approaching the batter's box, he bellowed out in a deep southern drawl, "Hey there, Wolff, y'all hit a homa' and I'll give y'all half the kitty!"

Well, the way my bank account was in need of a transfusion, I wanted that $35 as much as he did. I must have given him quite a thrill when, on the first pitch, I hit the line drive shot off the wall. I must have given the front office quite a scare, too. The way we've been drawing (or I should say, haven't been drawing) fans, $70 might have broken the Anderson franchise.

Anderson, S.C.
May 10

George Cappuzzello and I have been roommates for about a month now in our cozy little trailer and we have become good friends. As any married couple can tell you, I'm sure, you get to know a lot about a person when you live with him.

Cappy is quite a character, not eccentric, exactly, but unusual. First, it's an upset that he's even here. He was almost released in spring training, but they gave him a chance to pitch. He wasn't overpowering and he didn't have a great curve ball, but he just kept getting people out with an excellent change-up curve, a good head and almost perfect control. He is pitching well for us.

ge Cappuzzello, with whom I shared a
r overlooking a dump.

Cappy is a good guy and a good roommate, very easy to get along with. He's the kind of guy whose world revolves around baseball. The first thing he does when he gets up in the morning is read the sports pages and memorize everything, batting averages, standings. He knows all the statistics not only of all the ballplayers and teams in the major leagues, but of the minor leagues, as well.

His diet absolutely amazes me. He seems to subsist solely on soda pop and hamburgers, those big Whoppers you get at Burger King. I'm always amazed when Cappy has a pre-game meal of soda and hamburgers and then goes out and pitches a five-hitter or something.

Anderson, S.C.
May 12

For the past couple of weeks, I've been riding the pines, picking up splinters in my rear. In other words, I've been benched.

The combination of my batting average and the excellent play of Nat Calamis at second base is the reason I've had to take a front row center seat on the dugout bench. But just as I was falling deeper into the depths of despair, thinking how nice it would be to be in Cambridge for spring, my spirits were revived and my ego soared to the heights, proving, once again, that the life of a professional baseball player is one giant roller coaster.

We were playing Spartanburg on a typically hot and sunny Sunday afternoon in Anderson. The game was tied, 1–1, in the eighth inning and I was basking in the sun's rays, my mind drifting away when my reverie was rather brusquely interrupted. I had been called on to pinch-hit, theoretically to win the game for the A-Tigers. I was figuring all this out as I loosened up by swinging a few bats, but it still seemed a bit foggy in my dazed brain. Usually, when I'm called on to pinch-hit, a flash of adrenaline rushes through my frame and my entire body becomes acutely aware of what's going on.

46

As I dug in at home plate, I still couldn't figure out why I wasn't nervous. I felt as calm as if I were reading a book. There was no sensation of adrenaline or nervousness or anything, and, frankly, it frightened me. But I went through the motions of being a pinch-hitter, the ritual of swinging a weighted bat and wiping my hands on the pine tar rag and taking a few practice cuts, and as the paper reported, "Then with one out and Shortell on second base in the eighth inning, pinch-hitter Rick Wolff tripled to drive in Shortell with the go-ahead run."

It wasn't until I reached third that I finally realized what I had done. I was the hero. It was as simple as that. I had done what people, kids and fans, dream about doing—coming off the bench and delivering a clutch hit. Instantaneously, I love baseball, the fans are wonderful, life is golden and isn't this a lot of fun?

Remember in *Casey at the Bat,* the line that says, "Somewhere birds are singing and somewhere the sun is shining and somewhere children shout?" To me, that place today is right here in good old Anderson, South Carolina, USA!

Charleston, S.C.
May 16

This is our second trip here and I have found Charleston to be full of charm. Of course, there are some run-down places, but for the most part it's an intriguing city. For one thing, it's small and quaint, squeezed up against the ocean and full of cramped, cobblestone streets. Even more enticing are the palm trees that line the streets—just like being in Florida again.

The city is replete with Revolutionary and Civil War monuments and plaques, and in many ways Charleston reminds me very strongly of Boston. Except for the palm trees, of course.

To my greater delight, as Tis, Fern and I went sightseeing, we discovered an old museum right around the corner from our motel, a beautiful old white building done in antebellum style, as are most of the homes here.

We eagerly went inside and gazed for a couple of hours at the most wonderful collection of junk I have ever seen, everything from Civil War uniforms to Brazilian shrunken heads. It was quite a show.

At night we played the Charleston Pirates on their home field, which is known as College Park (it belongs to The Citadel, which is located in Charleston). My excitement continued to build, for this is a true stadium, enclosed by large cinder-block walls and bleachers able to hold thousands of people. Wow, I thought the first time I saw it, this is the big leagues.

Unfortunately, the field didn't measure up to the exterior surroundings. The dirt part of the infield was unique, at least to me, for I had never fielded a ground ball on seashells before. Generously speckled with bits and pieces of white chips, the infield looked like a reclaimed Atlantis.

To get used to this strange surface before the game, I decided to commit baseball's version of hara-kiri and asked one of the pitchers to hit me a few ground balls. After fending a dozen or so bad hops off my chest, neck, legs and other crucial parts of my body, I came to the astute conclusion that the field was, in its own way, something special.

The secret of playing here is purely mental. Just imagine you're enjoying a day at the beach and the rest comes easy. You can fool yourself into fielding grounders at Charleston just by playing your own shell game.

We won the game, 3–2, but I was hitless in four at-bats and made an error. Errors, I decided, hurt a lot more than hitless nights.

On this particular boot, I charged what appeared to be a normal, routine grounder. Just as I reached for it, it seemed to skip off the shells, glance off my glove, bounce off my chest and then I swear, hide from me as my panic-stricken fingers groped to dig it out of the low-tide debris around my feet.

I think the official scorer was waiting for this big moment. He was faster pressing the "E" button than I was finding the ball. There came the red glow on the scoreboard as the error sign sadistically mocked my effort.

No flash on and off, either. It lit up and stayed on for what seemed an eternity so that the whole world would know that I had been charged with an error.

Baseball is the only sport, probably the only profession in the world, where one's errors are announced, exhibited, displayed, printed and publicized so that everybody can laugh at you or curse you out.

En Route from Charleston to
Anderson
May 17

It was after midnight when we boarded our bus for the four-and-a-half-hour trip back to Anderson. It was not a pleasant thing to look forward to, but we had won two games, which made the trip less annoying.

I kept thinking about Harvard baseball bus rides to such remote places as Hanover, New Hampshire, and Princeton, New Jersey, when the guys just brought along their school books and read, a veritable library on wheels. The long, boring hours seemed like an eternity. A pitcher might be reading Pico della Mirandola's treatise "On The Dignity Of Man," while the shortstop was totally absorbed in his biochemistry of non-vertebrate animals. Educated, but boring.

As we left Charleston, we stopped at a red light, right next to a playground. It was midnight, but there were kids playing basketball. They were pretty good and most of the guys on the bus watched them as we waited for the light to change.

Suddenly and unexpectedly, Brian Sheekey, the resident bon vivant of the team, broke the silence with an amazingly good imitation of Marv Albert, the New York Knickerbockers' radio announcer. Doing the play-by-play of the playground game, Sheekey, in the distinct Albert nasal tone, had us completely enthralled.

"Frazier over to Monroe . . . back to Frazier . . . Clyde with a jumper from fifteen feet . . . YESSSSS . . . Knicks lead by 89–75, and now a word from Schaefer Beer . . ."

Instant insanity erupted. Since many of the guys on the team are from the New York area, Sheek's impersonation was an instant smash. The Sheek just ate up the attention and proceeded to entertain for the next two hours. His skits ran from imitations of Albert, George Carlin and Marlon Brando to a real novelty—a perfect impersonation of New York Mets announcer Bob Murphy, something that I'm certain had never been attempted before, anywhere. Sheekey was just great.

Then, when the Sheek ran out of steam, Steve Tissot took over. Tis, a veteran pitcher and self-appointed team philosopher, brought out his guitar and went through a wide range of songs. Everybody joined in, the extinct Singing Senators being reincarnated in the form of the Tuneful Tigers.

When this got a little boring, Steve Litras, our third baseman and a Groucho Marx freak, grabbed a pair of glasses, messed his hair, put a black comb over his upper lip, struck a cigar in his mouth and walked up and down the aisle in typical Grouchoesque fashion.

For the grand finale, as the bus entered into the town of Anderson after four in the morning, Tissot struck up the popular tune, "Yellow Submarine" and Sheekey was the band leader. They started marching up and down the aisle and everybody was singing and clapping along with them. We kept it up until everybody had filed out of the bus in the cold, dark, quiet Anderson Stadium parking lot.

A visit to Greenwood means an opportunity to see the legendary knuckleballer Hoyt Wilhelm, who manages the Greenwood team. Hoyt is something of an enigma, especially to those of us who grew up following his career. And who didn't? He had such a long career.

Wilhelm doesn't have much to say and he usually pitches batting practice to his players. He seems to enjoy baffling his own players with his unbelievable knuckleball in batting practice just as much as he enjoyed baffling big-league hitters when he was an active player.

I decided to go behind the batting cage and look at Wilhelm work, just to get an idea of what it was like to hit against him. It didn't take me long to realize how difficult he must have been and why he was so successful. The impression I got from watching him was that the ball was stationary and the scenery behind it was moving.

Steve Tissot, the club's Ol' Philosopher, is scheduled to pitch the second game of tonight's doubleheader against Greenwood.

Tis is one of a kind and he personifies the crafty veteran and voice of experience for most of the players. He's older than most of us, almost twenty-six, has been through the University of Delaware and has experienced the ups and downs of professional baseball.

Tis has long straggly blond hair that yearns to be longer and his face, although friendly, would probably be more comfortable if it were covered by a beard. His story follows a trend of the times: A pre-business major, he decided to kick all of his materialistic training and take up his true passion, the guitar. How he ended up in baseball, I'm still not certain.

Yet Tis is now an expert guitarist with a large and eclectic repertoire. He enjoys the transient life of a ballplayer and is the possessor of a goofy, but likable smile. Every so often he will transform a simple sneeze into a dramatic convolutional performance that builds into a suspenseful crescendo, finally satisfying not only him but all of his anticipating audience.

A few years back, Tis was in AA ball at Montgomery, where he was considered an outstanding prospect. He set a few strikeout records. Then he developed arm trouble, which explains his presence in Anderson. He has pitched against many players now in the major leagues, lending credence to his word on pitching matters. Steve speaks with authority, but often in mystical prose. When one of the local sportswriters asked him why he was so successful in Anderson even though he no longer had a blazing fastball, Tis replied, in true Descartian fashion, "I think, therefore I am."

Most pitchers get very tense before a game, but Tis doesn't. Unlike most pitchers, he has his own theories on pregame training meals and diet. He doesn't believe in big pregame meals; in fact, he doesn't believe in small ones, either.

On game days, Tis eats nothing but candy bars. He fasts until mid-afternoon, then he makes a purchase of nine or ten candy bars of assorted sizes in the local candy store and begins to munch his way voraciously into preparation for the night's encounter.

Tis is a firm believer that quick energy is the secret to maintaining a live fastball and a hard, sharp-breaking slider. When explaining his theory, Tis says the carbohydrates in the candy are broken down by his gastrointestinal system into individual saccharide compounds, thereby producing an infinite and instant source of energy, and as the mitochondria in the muscle cells of his pitching arm metabolize the glucose, the ATP is transformed into ADP, leaving diphosphate available to dispose of the lactic acid that builds up from muscular exhaustion. After that kind of explanation, all one can do is nod in agreement.

Now, Tis has been the candy man for years and it always works, he says, so nobody argues with him. His eating pace really gets into high gear about a half hour before the game. All you can see is Tis stuffing candy bars into his mouth.

There are serene moments in Tis' preparation, too. As the game gets closer, all the guys are out taking batting practice and the locker room gets quiet except for a few scattered bugs crawling around.

At this time, Tis can be found in his cubicle, reading. This is not unusual, until you look at what he's reading. There is Tis, about to go out and pitch a game in the Class A Western Carolinas league, soaking up the most profound philosophical treatises ever written. On one occasion I found him reading some stuff by the German philosopher Nietzsche on the meaning of life.

On another occasion, I found him reading Hermann Hesse's *Siddhartha* and *Steppenwolf,* some of the most difficult texts ever to be tackled in collegiate English courses.

Before tonight's first game, Tis and I were fielding ground balls together. Steve fancies himself a potentially great, if undiscovered, third-baseman. We got talking about famous books in American literature, not an uncommon topic for us. Every so often, one of us would ask the other if he recalled some famous line from a particular book or play, and we kept quizzing each other back and forth.

I asked Tis what the last line of *The Great Gatsby* was and he immediately broke into a grin that meant he knew the answer. But he stammered. He couldn't recall it for the moment. He groped and struggled, trying to come up with the answer, but he couldn't. I had to take infield practice, so I walked off, confident I had stumped him.

Between games, I asked Tis if he had it yet. He said he was still working on it, piecing it together bit by bit, and promised he would eventually get the whole thing.

I didn't know how he would be able to concentrate on pitching the second game and trying to remember the quote, but I learned some time ago never to underestimate my pal Tis.

The second game began and Tis was in control of things, but we weren't giving him many runs. We were leading, 3–2, in the top of the seventh when Steve began to tire a little. He walked the leadoff batter and the next guy bunted him over to second. Now Greenwood's best hitter was up. Tis had no problem with him earlier in the game, but it was decided to walk him intentionally and set up a double play.

Things got more tense as Tis fell behind, 2–0, on the batter. With the pressure mounting, Tis stepped off the rubber, fidgeted with his belt, then called time out and walked off the mound in my direction. I figured he wanted to work a pick off or maybe he just wanted to catch his breath.

I trotted in from second and as I approached the mound, Tis' eyes lit up, that smile came back to his face, and the first words out of his mouth were, "So we beat on, boats against the current, borne back ceaselessly into the past."

He had it, the last line of *The Great Gatsby*. Now, smugly, he stepped back on the mound, got the batter to hit into a double play and we won the game, 3–2.

Greenwood, S.C.
May 23

The Greenwood games are broadcast, both home and away, and since Greenwood is only a short distance from Anderson, the Greenwood announcer, Larry Gar, has become quite a celebrity, especially with the Anderson Tigers.

Gar's broadcast booth is perched on top of the covered stands in Greenwood, and like a squawking mother hen, Larry tries to run the entire affair as though it were his center stage performance. The broadcast is incidental to his act. He liberally spikes all his comments with biting humor about every player on our team. No one is ignored.

For nine innings, Larry will spice his play-by-play with painfully accurate descriptions of Sheekey's gut, Tissot's hair,

Nat Calamis' glasses, Hal Underwood's penchant for throwing errors and my balding head. On close calls that go against Greenwood, he will lean perilously out of the press booth and shout all kinds of barbs at the umpire, within hearing distance of the live microphone, of course. I heard that once when he got on Jimmy Piersall, Jim ran up to the booth and started strangling him while he was broadcasting a game. Somehow, I think Gar made that up.

One game earlier this month, we were still new to Gar and his antics, but Larry, a transplanted Brooklynite, proved he was a true New Yorker. Many of the Anderson players were from the New York area, so it was natural that almost all of us rooted for the New York Knickerbockers basketball team and were interested in the scores of the play-off games against the Lakers. We knew that Gar had access to a radio and was following the game as he did the play-by-play of the Greenwood-Anderson game.

During the fourth inning, with a lull in the action, Larry leaned out of his booth and yelled as loud as he could to our third-baseman, Steve Litras, who comes from Long Island.

"Hey, Stevie, the Knicks are up by thirteen at the end of the third quarter!"

At this intrusion in the ballgame, Okrie just about swallowed his wad of tobacco. Steve blushed a nice shade of crimson and Larry sported a wide, Cheshire-cat grin. Larry Gar had struck again!

Spartanburg, S.C.
May 24

Another set of statistics came out in today's paper. It amazes me how important these numbers are to pro ballplayers, for certainly a batting average or earned-run average cannot truly measure one's ability. Too many intangibles are unaccounted for, values that can't be measured by statistics but distinguish

55

ballplayers—like hustle and desire to win, giving oneself up for the betterment of the team and baseball savvy.

Everybody on the team will admit this, but at the same time they're figuring out their stats to make certain that the official scorer didn't rob them of a few precious batting average points.

I know all this is true because I've begun to think this way. I have been brainwashed by my batting average. I was lured away by the golden dream of becoming a .300 hitter and in so doing, I gave up my sanity. I hate to confess it, but I've become a batting average freak just like the rest of the team.

Over the last couple of weeks I've raised my batting average from .250 to .276. In fact, this distinct rise in my average is precisely why I've become this way; I'm starting to consciously chase that pot of gold at the end of the rainbow, the .300 mark. Yet as any Little Leaguer knows, points are easier to lose than to gain.

At the beginning of the season I had made a solemn oath that I would never worry about my stats. My rationale was as follows: Baseball is a nice job and I should enjoy myself; then, even if I don't do well and don't enjoy myself, I really shouldn't worry too much because I can always go back to school and graduate.

That was Harvard Rationale, not Major League Baseball Rationale. This thought process which I invented was done with a cool, composed mind. Unfortunately, it did not take into account the highly emotional, choleric and heathen attitude of a ballplayer going 0–for–5. Since this important factor was left out, my rationale didn't survive the first week.

This entire concern with stats, unbeknownst to laymen, leads to an incredible sociological phenomenon—the Worship of the God of Hits. Many ballplayers are inevitably irreverent and blasphemous when it comes to religion, but when they discuss their batting average they become as pious as monks. The God of Hits is a god of extremes—he is either extremely benevolent or extremely harsh. Each ballplayer usually has his own individual ritual that he employs to elicit the kindness of the god, wearing a good-luck charm, repetition of some action, saying magic words before he bats, and so on. If the god is pleased, he rewards the individual with a hit every night. In essence, the ballplayer lives for a 1–for–4 every night and hopes that every so often, the god will be especially pleased and reward him by granting him a 2–for–4.

Anderson, S.C.
May 25

Every so often I pick up a newspaper and read in some sports page about a phenomenal sports performance. Or I'll peruse an old *Sports Illustrated,* turn to the back and glance at their "Faces in the Crowd" section. There, like millions of other sports-crazed Americans, I'll read in astonishment how some Joe Schmoe scored eighteen touchdowns in one game or threw twelve no-hitters while batting .895. Like millions of others, I quickly scoff at such nonsense, relying on my common sense to remind me that such things are not possible.

Tonight, however, did a lot to change my views on such matters. Good ol' country boy, Al Newsome, who has been struggling with curve balls all season and getting jammed when he guessed fast ball, put on a show I'm certain will not be matched for quite some time. Like so many other sober and respectable Americans who have seen UFOs, I was actually present, both sober and respectable, at Mr. Newsome's fireworks.

Let me quote from the newspaper account of the game: "Newsome put on the biggest display of power that has ever been witnessed here as he slammed three home runs and a double and drove in all seven runs in a 7–6 victory over the Spartanburg Phillies."

We were behind 4–0 in the second inning when Newsome

belted one over the left-field scoreboard with one on. After the Phillies made it 5–2, Newsome came back and hit a ball 410 feet over the center field fence to cut the margin to 5–4.

In the seventh inning, Newsome came up with two on and two out and blasted his third home run over the center field fence to give us a 7–5 lead.

Each home run was the kind of blast that enhances the legend. The second one was shot out of a cannon, clearing the center field fence right over the "Free Lt. Calley" sign and into the darkness. It was simply astounding. As they say, I would have liked to have chopped up that home run into a dozen singles.

After the game was over, something happened that pushed this game into the world of Ripley's "Believe It Or Not." In appreciation of what our mighty slugger had accomplished, the Anderson fans passed the hat and came up with more than $100, which they gave to Big Al. These people had already paid their way in, yet they were so thrilled by Newsome's performance that they dug down and chipped in although many of them don't make as much money as we do.

I was also present when Harvard tied Yale, 29–29, a few years back, scoring sixteen points in the last forty-two seconds. Nobody passed a hat that day.

Greenwood, S.C
June 1

The stats came out again today and I'm hanging in there very satisfactorily at a .278 pace. I still have my sights set on the .300 mark, but I'll certainly settle for a cozy .280. After all, figure a first year pro who plays tough second base and hit .280 is a good, solid prospect. Of course, we still haven't finished the first half of the season, but if I can just keep getting my one hit per game for the rest of the season, I'll end up just fine. Just one hit a game. It sounds so easy.

58

The team is rambling along with a 23–21 record thanks to a recent seven game winning streak. It's good enough for third place in the league, only five games out of first. We're still within striking distance of Gastonia, but the first half comes to a close next week, so our chances are dimming each day. But with all the close games we lost and the tough breaks we've had, we're not doing too badly.

I was thinking we've played forty-four games already and we still have three months ahead of us. I have actually played a full season and more, for no college team I ever played on ever had more than thirty-five games on its schedule. Now, as a pro, I still have over ninety games left before I can go home.

I've been playing ball every day since February and, frankly, I'm getting a bit tired and lonely. I never thought I would say this, but baseball games have become somewhat routine, just like going to work every day.

February, March, April, May and now June. Even the pre-game music at the Anderson ballpark is becoming increasingly tedious. It's Herb Alpert and his Tijuana Brass every night. I can imagine a scene twenty years from now when I'm long past my baseball days and I'm at a ritzy dinner party and all of a sudden the orchestra starts playing "The Spanish Flea." Just like an operant-conditioned Skinnerian rat, I'll probably start sweating uncontrollably, begin to spout all sorts of foulmouthed baseball language, and then, in an involuntary spastic fit, signal the orchestra leader to hit me a few grounders.

Anderson, S.C.
June 8

This was one of the most disappointing days in my life. Let me explain. My girl friend Linda, who had just graduated from Radcliffe, came down for a short visit.

Linda had never seen me play baseball before. In college, she concentrated in Fine Arts and was pre-med, and this left her little time to learn the game of baseball. As a result, Linda could not, and probably never would, fully understand why I decided to leave her, Harvard and all the comforts of Cambridge to pursue some childhood ambition. At this particular moment, I share her feeling.

At the start of the week, I welcomed the opportunity to show Linda what I had been doing in my baseball career. I was fully determined to give her some insight into the world of professional baseball, with an emphasis on my talent. Somehow I felt compelled to convince her why I had left her in February and to show her that my efforts were worthwhile and exciting. I wanted to show her the glamor of a pro ballplayer in a small town. I wanted to plant the thought in her mind that I was doing well. And most importantly, I wanted her to realize that I had made a wise and valuable choice.

As it turned out, it was a very inauspicious showing. In fact, it was a nightmare. In baseball, only the unpredictable is predictable, and this week was no exception.

After going three weeks without a rain-out, it rained. For three straight days. I anxiously awaited the next day to bring back that glorious southern sunshine just so I could show dear Linda what baseball in the minor leagues is all about.

My prayers were answered! Today was a simply beautiful, brilliant, sunshiny day. But by the time 7:00 P.M. had rolled around, the rain clouds had also rolled around. By game time, there was a fine mist in the air, thousands of little particles of raindrops forming mini-rainbows in the bright lights of the stadium. Linda found herself a seat about ten rows back, which wasn't hard to do because there were only about fifty people in the stands, and had covered herself with a raincoat and umbrella.

60

Yet this was the time of reckoning, time to rise to the occasion, for this might be my only chance to prove my worth as a ballplayer to Linda.

Attired in my resplendent white home uniform, I fancied myself as the gallant Prince Charming marching onto the field of battle and readying myself to repel these evil and malevolent intruders from afar, the Spartanburg Phillies. Behold, the lovely lady has spotted me, and waved to me oh, so gracefully. Enthralled by her beauty, I immediately doffed my cap and humbly bowed. Upon rising, I declared, "Fear not my lady-ship, for I, with the aid of my trusty Louisville Slugger, will go forth and do battle with these foul-mouthed, tobacco-spewing barbaric brutes."

After uttering these chivalrous words, I went onto the field fully anticipating a glorious night of victory. By this time, the fine mist, which had given everything in the ballpark a spiritually romantic quality, had now become a wet and grubby drizzle, instantly washing away any traces of beauty, and portending ominous things.

It rained, not drizzle or mist, but actually rained for the entire game, all nine miserable innings.

The leadoff batter, innocently enough, walked. The next batter singled. The third batter hit a double play ball, but the shortstop slipped in the mud and threw the ball away. The next guy hit one off the wall and from then on, an avalanche of hits, walks and errors resulted in Phillie runs . . . ten of them before we got anybody out. I still don't believe it happened.

That put a quick end to thoughts of a team triumph, but if I were able to get a couple of hits, that would salvage something from this miserable night. But when it was all over, we had lost, 13–1, I had gone 0–for–4 and Linda was busily packing to return to Boston wondering, no doubt, just why I was wasting my time.

Anybody who has ever gone to a baseball game is aware of that infamous man in blue, that seemingly innocent bystander who somehow becomes the focal point of every argument on the field. They may be in the right or they may be totally wrong, but one has to face the facts, you just can't have a baseball game without umpires.

There have been countless spoofs, parodies and satires written about umpires through the ages, how they inevitably suffer from myopia and how they incur the wrath of the fans when they blow a close play, and how they have extremely low boiling points which, when reached, result in the ejection of an argumentative and vociferous player.

My academic interest being in psychology, I have always found umpires to be a curious breed. To be precise, after long hours of clinical examination, I consider umpires to be classic case studies of the sado-masochistic character.

The umpire has to enjoy being a power symbol. The game cannot start, even if both teams are ready, until the umpire shows up. The umpire determines what baseballs are used, what pitches are strikes and balls, when enough rain has fallen to stop a game, when a ball is fair or foul, when a player or manager has argued too much or said the wrong thing.

Practically every important decision is made by the umpires. This desire to rule over others and to have one's verdict stand as law is very typical of the sadistic character (see Erich Fromm's *The Anatomy of Human Destructiveness*).

Yet just when the umpire appears to have reached a full and unquestioned control over all others, his dictatorial role can be vehemently challenged. I've seen half-crazed maniacal managers rush up to umpires to question their judgment, jaw at them at a rather intimate distance, and purposely slur over

62

their diction in order to punctuate their points with a well-aimed spray of tobacco juice. Even batters who are barely hitting their weight will occasionally turn on umpires by questioning their calls on certain pitches. The umpires respond in a battle to maintain their authority and self-control. They always are sure of the last word, which is "out," accompanied by a thumb in the air.

But despite their abnormal psychological leanings, one must not forget that umpires are human and that they will, sometimes, make mistakes. I've tried to remind them of this on occasion, but few care to admit during a game that, like others, they too are fallible.

Dave Slickenmeyer is a large, loud-mouthed pompous individualist. In other words, he's a good umpire. I made the mistake of questioning his judgment and I lived to regret it. He didn't purposely make calls against me—he's got too much class for that—he'd simply strike up a conversation with me while the pitcher was winding up and I was in the box, concentrating on the pitch.

Do you have any idea how irritating it is to have somebody talk to you while you're trying to bat? I know darn well Slick doesn't care where my home town is, nor for my opinion of Watergate. But since I haven't got ear plugs, I am forced to listen and as I strike out swinging, I just walk back to the bench saying, "Damn you, Slick, why don't you just shut up and let me hit?"

"But Rick," the big baboon smilingly yells back at me, "I was just trying to be friendly."

Gastonia, N.C.
June 16

The Harvard class of '73 graduated today. On this memorable day in my life, I, Richard Hugh Wolff, Harvard '73, was going 0–for–5. A very sobering, almost depressing thought, indeed.

On the two-hour bus ride here I was thinking a lot about missing what was to have been my graduation. I could easily see myself and my college buddies, all together again at Mather House, drinking champagne, partying, reminiscing about our years at Harvard. I let my dreams run wild, as I am apt to do on long bus rides. I envisioned that when we got to Gastonia, right before the game started, right before the national anthem, the public address announcer, unbeknownst to me and everyone in the stands, would address the crowd in the following manner:

"Ladies and gentlemen, we would like to take this time to extend our congratulations and best wishes to the Anderson second-baseman, Rick Wolff, upon his graduation from Harvard College, magna cum laude, on this sixteenth of June, nineteen hundred and seventy-three."

My fantasy continued and I saw in my mind's eye the crowd rising in solemn tribute to me, completely in awe of my academic status. With the sun shining brilliantly, just beginning to regain consciousness, the inspiring martial tones of the famous Harvard fight song, "10,000 Men of Harvard," would blast throughout the small ballpark, followed by the national anthem. It would be simply great.

The bus rambled on and then it stopped for our pre-game meal. Instinctively, I recalled pre-game meals at Harvard, where on the day of the contest we would all solemnly enter the Harvard Varsity Club, plush, well-furnished, thoroughly drenched in Harvard athletic history. Every famous athlete or famous athletic event that had involved Harvard had his or its picture on the wall. And then we lined up for the meal. Everybody got a thick steak with baked potato, vegetables, salad, pancakes, ice cream with chocolate sauce.

My reverie was punctuated when I noticed the familiar orange arch of McDonald's. I ordered a cheeseburger, French fries and a Coke.

Our game was delayed tonight for over a half hour. A stray cat was giving birth to a litter of kittens out in right field. Everybody on both teams gathered around for the blessed event, although I don't think the mother cat appreciated the attention.

I had heard of guys getting married at baseball games, but this was going a bit too far.

Coming into tonight's game, our pitching staff was working on a streak of three shutout games in a row, which had tied the Western Carolinas record. Bob Shortell was pitching, shooting for the record. He got all the way to the ninth inning when, with one out, he threw a hanging curve ball to a Gastonia batter named Mike Hargrove, who hit it approximately 420 feet over the right-center field fence, ending our shutout streak at thirty-two innings. At least we won the game, 3–1.

I watched the Rangers go through their usual pre-game in-field/outfield routine. It certainly is a strange one.

Coach Ed Nottle was trying to sharpen the accuracy of Gastonia's outfielders. His method of instruction was rather novel.

First he put on all the catcher's gear, including shin guards, chest protector, mask and, I assume, a protective cup. Then he strapped a supplementary mask around his groin area for added protection. Thus armored, he took the position of cut-off man for the outfielders' throws and the purpose of the drill, honestly, was to have the Gastonia outfielders "hit the cut-off man." Literally.

Unflinchingly, Nottle stood his ground while players gleefully tried to throw their hardest and most accurate shots right at him. A couple of the throws came pretty close. In fact, one of them went right through his legs. Fortunately for Nottle, Gastonia has some fairly inaccurate outfielders.

Anderson, S.C.
June 23

Luis Atilano's parents came all the way from Puerto Rico to see him play tonight.

It was a very dramatic setting, enhanced by Wilfred Binette, who is the sportswriter and columnist of the Anderson *Daily Mail,* the official scorer, the public address announcer in the Anderson ballpark and the emcee for all sports activities in Anderson.

When Luis, our tall, skinny first baseman, came to bat his first time, Wilfred set the stage by announcing that Looie's mom and dad had come from Puerto Rico.

Looie stepped out of the batter's box as the people in the ballpark gave his parents a warm ovation. Then Luis moved back in, got set and on the first pitch planted one over the Pepsi-Cola sign way out in left center—a home run. It was unbelievable. Nobody has his parents introduced and then hits a home run on the first pitch. He hadn't hit more than two or three homers all year and he does this. I was so happy for Looie and for his proud parents, but if I ever saw something like that in a movie, I'd never go for it. Too unrealistic.

Anderson, S.C.
June 24

The size and nature of the crowds that attend our home games vary with each game. Yet, as the season progresses, it is in-

agine, Luis Atilano hit a homer on the day his
rents came from Puerto Rico to see him.

creasingly evident that some of the fans are loyal, true-blue Anderson rooters who come to every game no matter the weather, the opposition or our position in the standings. They're a mixed bunch, farmers with their families, teen-aged girls, widowed housewives, old men who reminisce of days gone by and few local characters who play loud roles in the stands as hecklers, noisemakers, umpire baiters or all-knowing strategists.

It's not unusual to hear someone cheer for a favorite player and to see that player acknowledge his backer with a tip of the cap. Attachments are formed, fan for player, player for fan.

One day, I was playing pepper in front of the stands. At one point, the ball went over the railing right in front of an elderly black gentleman. I went to retrieve the ball (in the minors the fans give the balls back) and the man eagerly picked up the baseball and with an awkward motion that exuded age and arthritis, tossed it back to me.

A little later, the ball went back in his direction again and I went to retrieve it. This time I made some comment to the old man about my obvious lack of skill as a pepper player, and he just leaned forward on his wooden cane and laughed a deep cackle. As he smiled, he exposed the only couple of teeth left in his head and I realized that he must have been very old indeed. His dark, black skin covered his bony frame tightly and his hands were gnarled like the branches of an oak tree. His face was friendly and covered with a peach-like white fuzz of whiskers.

Before I could get back to the game, the old man started talking baseball, about whom he had seen play here in years past, about his days as a player, who his favorite player was and so on. He just rambled on, enjoying himself and pulling out memories as fast as he could. Finally, I excused myself and he urged me to play well and win.

Later, I did some investigating about him. I found out

that he had been to every home game for over fifteen years. I heard he had also been a pretty fair pitcher back in his youth, playing in the "colored leagues" and was still revered around the area as a "local Satchel Paige."

Last night we played Gastonia and the old man was there in his customary seat. Around the third inning, there was a stir in the stands, but since I was out in the field and concentrating on the game, I couldn't really make out what was going on. But as the third out was recorded, we came hustling off the field and I could see the old man crouching over, his hand on his left side. There was a painful look on his face, the most agonizing look I have ever seen. His cane had fallen to the ground and he was gasping for breath. Around him some of the fans, mostly black, were in a panic. One woman was crying uncontrollably and a few younger men were running up the stadium steps, no doubt going for help.

It was an awful moment in my life. I felt helpless and unbelievably guilty as the ambulance squad came by and took the old man away. The game continued, but I couldn't do a thing to help the old man—I could only stand there and watch. I felt cold all over. I had to concentrate on winning a minor league baseball game, which suddenly seemed dreadfully unimportant, even sacrilegious.

Today a public address announcement said the old man had been to every home game for so many years and that he had died last night. I didn't feel like playing, but the game went on.

Charleston, S.C.
June 27

Something unusual always seems to happen when we go to Charleston and this last trip was no exception. Saturday night was a big promotional night for the Pirates and they had a five-piece rock band playing before the game. The ballpark, which seats about 9,000, was packed to the rafters. In fact, there seemed to be a few thousand standees cluttering the aisles and searching frantically for a seat.

Everybody was having a good time. The band happened to be really top-notch and the ballpark was rocking. Many of the fans were drinking beer and singing and dancing, really enjoying themselves. Even Sheek was dancing a little jig out in the outfield. And the fans didn't want the band to stop playing. They insisted that the game be delayed and the group allowed to continue.

But the Pirate management naturally wouldn't hear of this, and so the band came to a sudden halt while the umpire and managers gathered at home plate to exchange line-up cards. Disgruntled, the fans who had been chanting for more music decided to sit and judge the caliber of the ballgame for a while, or possibly just went out to get more beer. All of a sudden, around the middle of the second inning, we were at bat when we noticed that, up in the stands, some spectators were having some sort of disagreement.

Disagreements are not uncommon in minor league audiences—or major league audiences, for that matter—but it is rare when one of the participants decides to punctuate his point of view by smashing a folding chair over his counterpart's head. Responding to this outburst, the attacked participant retaliated by throwing his container of beer in his assailant's face. One thing led to another and suddenly, in a chain reaction, a whole section of the stands seemed to be involved, on the verge of a full-fledged riot.

The game quickly became embarrassingly meaningless. How can one possibly concentrate on playing baseball when, only a few feet away, people are screaming, shoving and mauling, beer cans are flying, police are blowing whistles, sirens are heard in the distance and the PA announcer is unsuccessfully pleading with the spectators to calm down? I didn't have much time to maintain my role of observer, for somebody on our team yelled and, turning around, I noticed that hundreds of kids were swarming over our dugout like ants at a picnic and grabbing anything that wasn't tied down.

All I could see were kids running off with Anderson baseball caps, batting helmets, bats, gloves and so on. The team had quickly dispersed in all directions, chasing little thieves, in desperate hope of recapturing personal equipment. Luckily, I was carrying my glove, but my next thought was for my bat. I ran over to the bat rack. Through the wire mesh fence, myriad little hands were reaching for bats and once they were held, they were instantly swooped up and pulled through the fence.

I ran to the fence in time to see half of my bat being swallowed by these hands. I grabbed on to the barrel and before I knew it, I had engaged myself in a serious tug-of-war over my property. Struggling with a multi-headed and anonymous enemy, I persevered until I won the contest. It was quite an effort, too, for those little kids formed a pretty strong force.

Having saved my bat, I clutched it to my glove and my cap and ran into the clubhouse. Inside, I found about a third of my teammates, all wielding bats as potential weapons, and telling stories of who had stolen their property and how. We waited there, gabbing about the "Battle of Charleston," until the rumbles outside died down and it seemed safe enough to come out and survey the ruins. The fans were returning to their seats apparently none the worse for their exertions, their emotions spent and their anger subsided. The rock band had packed its instruments and was gone. We warmed up for a few minutes again, almost as if there had been no interruption.

It was a big night in Charleston. A band concert, some of the best fighting seen outside of Madison Square Garden, a ballgame which turned out to be a home town victory and an overflow crowd to take in this variety show. Who says baseball isn't an action-packed, exciting sport?

We had the dubious pleasure of trying to hit against Lafayette Currence tonight. Currence, one of the hardest throwers in the league, "came out smoking," humming his way toward a no-hitter.

In my first at-bat, I succumbed to his overpowering velocity, swinging at a bad pitch and striking out. My second at-bat was a different story.

In Charleston, the box seats are close to the field and batter's box. As I approached my second turn at bat, some guy yelled out my name. Being a total professional, I ignored him and his pleas, but finally he was so persistent that I turned to see what was so urgent. The man was stunned when I acknowledged his presence and he began to stutter, finally stammering out the information that Currence could be bunted on. I waved and gave his idea some consideration.

I looked at the second-baseman, who was way back on the outfield grass, and decided to lay one down. To my amazement, I pushed an excellent bunt between first and second and Currence must have admired it, too, for he was late covering first. I was on first with a hit, the first hit of the game for Anderson. I glanced up at Benedict Arnold in the box seat. He was elated, simply ecstatic, obviously bragging smugly to his friends what great baseball acumen he possessed and what a great coach he'd make.

I eventually came around to score and as I passed the man, he got up and gave me a one-man standing ovation.

Fern Poirier "died" today.

Everybody just sort of stopped what he was doing and hung his head in a moment of silence when the news was heard. Fern, one of our outfielders, had just been released.

72

In baseball, when a player is released or traded, his team-mates say he "died."

For a while, nobody said anything. Very quitely, Fern walked over to his open wooden locker, took off his bag and began to pack his things. In a few minutes, he had finished—all that remained in his locker was the Anderson uniform—and Fern started making the rounds, saying his goodbyes to his teammates. Then he picked up his baseball bag and sto-ically walked out of the clubhouse door—and out of our lives.

Tis came over and asked, "Why Fern? He was just be-ginning to get going, starting to hit the ball well."

Jeff Natchez, our center fielder, sat on the clubhouse bench and shook his head. "Gee, he was such a nice guy. How come they released him?"

There was no answer. One minute Fern is a professional baseball player, laughing and joking and as loose as a ball-player should be, and the next minute Len Okrie asks him to step into his office and, suddenly, Fern's dream of becoming a major leaguer has ended.

Getting released, like dying, is inevitable. Still, it's tough to endure. How do you go home in the middle of the season and tell your friends you just weren't good enough? It's hard to admit to your friends. It's even harder to admit it to yourself.

Greenwood—Anderson, S.C.
July 4

What I had originally thought would be a lot of fun turned out to be a baseball marathon. The Fourth of July was always fun when I was a kid—fireworks, baseball games, picnics. And I looked forward to the celebration this year and the unique day-night doubleheader, home and home with the Greenwood club.

Last night's game ended around 10:30 and Harry Schulz, our somewhat corpulent trainer and surrogate mother figure, wrote the agenda for the next day on the blackboard. It didn't

73

take long for us to realize that holiday day-night doubleheaders might not be as much fun as we thought.

Our schedule called for us to be packed and ready to go to Greenwood by 10:00 A.M. for the afternoon game, which was to start at noon. Then we would return to Anderson to play at night.

The weather was unbelievable. It was, quite simply, the hottest day of the year and in South Carolina when it's hot, it's hot. The mercury soared past 100 degrees early in the morning.

By the time we disembarked from the bus in Greenwood, not one of the guys had a dry shirt on. Some guys stripped down and jumped in the shower, but it was to no avail. I sat there on the locker-room bench and watched the beads of perspiration roll off my body. My sweat glands were working overtime. But the worst was yet to come. We still had to go out and play not one, but two games in this tropical climate.

On hot days such as this one, and when one is playing at an opponent's field, the minor leaguer is obliged to wear his gray uniform. We don't have the luxury of the cooler double-knits the big leaguers use. The minor leaguer's gray uniform is always, without exception, made of a barbaric combination of agonizing wool and heat-retaining cotton, with a strong accent on the wool.

How can I describe the feeling? Maybe something like putting on a potato sack that is infested with thousands of sharp, prickling pins. Or a thick, stifling overcoat made of cactus and porcupine needles? People are always talking about all sorts of inhumane torture techniques; they ought to try a gray uniform in hot weather. It makes the Chinese water torture a welcome relief.

Once garbed in our pressure-cooker pin cushions, we ventured out onto the field of battle experiencing the kind of heat that makes you squint as the sweat continually stings your eyes. It's so hot that your spikes start to sizzle and smoke. Of course, the Greenwood players feel pretty much the same way

74

we do. It seemed to be the longest nine-inning game ever played.

When the game ended, we all showered, which had the total effect of just letting us sweat some more, and trucked back to Anderson. That hiatus proved to be the high point of the day, as the local fans had arranged a small feast for the ballplayers at the stadium. Not surprisingly, their supply of Coke, iced tea and lemonade was quickly consumed. Yet it seemed that as soon as we finished our dinner, it was time to play ball again and sweat some more.

The heat had abated somewhat, cooling down to a frigid 98 degrees. By the fourth inning, I started to have hallucinations. I'm certain I spotted Lawrence of Arabia eating popcorn in the stands down the first-base line. I went over to tell Sheekey my discovery, but he had formulated his own theory on the heat wave. He was babbling about the fact that there must be a nuclear war going on somewhere and the omnipresent heat we were experiencing was a direct result.

Meanwhile, some of the guys were spraying each other with some of the trainer's ethyl chloride to keep cool. I tried to warn them it probably wasn't too healthy, but they ignored me. Jack Walsh came in from the bullpen saying that some of the guys down there were tottering on the brink of heat exhaustion.

Unfortunately, there was one cold feature of the day and night—our bats. We lost both games, 4–3 and 5–3. Somehow, that always makes it seem even hotter.

Orangeburg, S.C.
July 8

There may be great beauty in Orangeburg, but one doesn't encounter it on the way to the ballpark.

A visit there can evoke instant depression. Run-down dwellings, broken windows, caved-in porches, weeds, litter— these are sights that greet you on the bus ride. Yet, incongruously, there are a couple of colleges on the outskirts of town with campuses that appear cared for, and there's a Holiday Inn that we stay at that is clean and new.

The baseball park, home of the Orangeburg Cardinals, is a battered structure. The stands are old and creaky, chipped planks with jagged splinters. A wire mesh screen, sagging and full of holes, makes a mockery of protection for the spectator.

On the field, however, one senses a spirit that belies the surroundings. There's an intensity to the warm-ups of the Orangeburg team. Their manager, Jimmy Piersall, is hitting grounders, yelling infield directions, and putting as much verve into every swing as if this were the World Series. About twenty fans focused their attention on the former big leaguer and they seemed to view his vitality as a source of amusement.

Occasionally on a lumpy field, a hard grounder would skip off an infielder's chest or over his shoulder. This would provoke gales of laughter from the early arrivals.

The most memorable characteristic of the Orangeburg ballpark lies just beyond the outfield fence. Here are the railroad tracks which occupy a unique part in the strategy of the game.

On most fields, there is usually a dark green backdrop in center field. The batter can focus on the white baseball in the contrast of colors. In Orangeburg, no such backdrop exists. The background consists of moving trains, complete with multicolored box cars that provide a kaleidoscopic effect upon the batter's eyes. The whole setup makes batting at Orangeburg a new and unique challenge.

Not surprisingly, the Cardinals have a pretty good pitching staff. Their pitchers simply turn around on the mound and face the outfield wall, waiting for some light colored box cars to come into sight. Then they time their actions, finally wind up and release their pitch just as the cars form a snow-like background for the helpless batter. More often than not, the batter swings pathetically at a meaningless box car insignia.

When we arrived for a series of games with the Cardinals, they had lost fifteen straight. Could the railroad have been on strike?

Hal Underwood led off for us in the top of the first and struck out just as a freight train was passing. As Hal walked back to the bench, I asked him what kind of pitch he struck out on.

Hal thought for a moment, then replied. "He got me on a sharp-breaking Penn Central refrigerated boxcar."

Anderson, S.C.
July 11

Occasionally a traveling salesman comes to the park, usually selling baseball equipment or possibly an encyclopedia or life insurance policies. We all gather around the guy and Len Okrie introduces him. He has about five minutes to make his pitch before the players start losing interest.

In most cases, only the bonus babies can afford to buy equipment or encylopedias, and since there is a paucity of bonus babies on the Anderson team, the salesmen rarely make many sales here.

This evening we had a salesman peddling a new product. He was selling pre-written term papers to prospective college students.

I was stunned. I couldn't believe the scruples of this salesman. All of my morals and ethics concerning schoolwork were being blatantly destroyed. What was even more disconcerting was that some of my teammates were intently listening to the guy.

After he gave his little spiel, I felt compelled to say something to somehow save my teammates' souls from the temptation of the devil. I kept listening, hoping to catch the salesman on a slip-up in reasoning or something.

"Excuse me, sir," I said, "but I think your product is great and a tremendous time-saver in college. I go to Harvard,

77

you see, and even in the Ivy League athletes are pressed for time with their tough schedules and term paper assignments. In fact, I know of an All-American football player, who just didn't have time to write a paper because of his tough football schedule, so he used a term paper service just like yours to get out of his bind."

At this point I paused, watching the salesman puff with pride after my apparent endorsement of his product.

"Unfortunately," I continued, "the term paper that my buddy handed in was recognized by the professor as being totally lifted out of a magazine article. They kicked my friend out of school for plagiarism."

I had hoped to tarnish his product sufficiently to discourage some of my teammates and, sure enough, most of them sort of laughed nervously and walked off. Yet, a few of them stayed on, perhaps fascinated by the salesman's brazenness.

As I warmed up for the game, I kept thinking of the *Damn Yankees* movie and the old ballplayer who reclaimed his youth by making a pact with the devil. I wondered if the demon with the horns had a few apprentices posing as salesmen getting their training, just like us, in the minor leagues.

Anderson, S.C.
July 12

The entire team was given ballots to pick this year's all-star team. The rules were fairly simple. You couldn't choose a player from your own team.

The selecting made for some interesting, and occasionally heated, discussion as players differed on who were the best players in the league. In particular, many of the arguments eventually came down to a debate on the merits of statistics and just how good an index they were to the player's all-around ability. I found to my surprise that some of my teammates, especially the younger ones, put a great deal of weight on things like batting averages and won-lost pitching records.

Their rationale consisted of statements like, "You can't vote for that guy, he's only hitting .236." Or, "Sure the guy might have a good curve ball, but his record is only 5–5."

This kind of talk bothered me because it ignored the intangibles of the game. When you play baseball long enough or observe it for a long period of time, the game breaks down into finer, and more intriguing, components.

The average spectator who sees one or two games a year, goes to a game with the hope of seeing a lot of home runs or a no-hitter. All the other things, the so-called little things, are insignificant to him.

But when you become a true fanatic of the game and a true student of its artistry, a whole new world opens up that makes the entire game inherently vibrant, exciting and strategic.

The average fan in the stands sees the pitcher throw the ball and the batter try to hit it. The pitcher is good if he has a winning record and, accordingly, the hitter is good if he is hitting close to .300. It's as simple as that. But a real student of the game will view the game more deeply than the statistics.

I like to consider the game as a computerized program of playing percentages. Let's say I'm batting against a certain pitcher. When I walk up to the plate, my mind is whirling with past experiences and bits of information that I have stored on this pitcher. I'm instantly thinking, "What kind of pitches does this guy throw? What have I done against him in the past? Does he use his breaking stuff and experiment when he gets ahead of me in the count? Is he a smart pitcher? Does he try to hit corners? Is he a good fielder? Is he tired? What is he thinking about me? How did he get me out before?" Questions like these quickly run through my brain, all before any action takes place, and it truly makes a more exciting game of it.

I play second base much the same way. I have an internalized book, or program, on every ballplayer in the league. I take into consideration his batting stance, strength, speed,

WILFRID B

That outfield sure isn't AstroTurf, as grounds-
keeper Early Adger will attest.

the field condition, the wind, who's pitching for us, how that particular batter has been hitting recently against our pitching staff, and so on. Each hitter is different.

Results in baseball, then, are foregone conclusions. A good, smart pitcher instinctively knows as soon as he has released his pitch whether the batter will swing and miss it or line it off the left-center field wall. By the same token, a batter's eyes will light up when he sees the pitcher's mistake coming up to the plate.

The crowd will wildly applaud a great play by a second baseman who goes deep in the hole to field a ball and throws the runner out. What the crowd does not realize is that the second baseman was shading the hitter to hit in that direction in the first place, before the pitch was thrown, and that's what made the play possible.

To me, baseball breaks down into three parts—10 percent luck, 40 percent physical skill, 50 percent mental strategy. The thrill of outthinking a smart opponent is one of the fundamental joys of baseball. Somebody once described baseball as "chess with muscles." I don't think that's too far wrong.

So, it is my contention that statistics don't come close to measuring a player's value. If, out of every 100 at-bats, a hitter got lucky and picked up a mere five infield singles, he would raise his average from .250 to .300.

There are a lot of players in this league I respect, not because of their stats, but because their skill, talent and mentality make them outstanding players. My all-star selections would surprise a lot of people, but I have a hunch that by the end of the year, my picks may emerge as the top prospects.

Anderson, S.C.
July 14

This is Max Patkin night in Anderson Memorial Stadium. Max put on quite a show.

Max Patkin is a former pro player who has carved out a

baseball career for himself putting on comedy routines as an extra attraction at ballparks from coast to coast.

I was looking forward to his act. I figured that at the very least, it would be a welcome change of pace.

About an hour before the game, Max came into our locker room and addressed the team. He is an elongated man with a nervous air about him. He has long legs, long arms, a long neck and a rather large, protruding nose to go with his gangly frame. After briefing us on his act, and what he wanted us to do, Max proceeded to change into his working clothes. He pulled the grubbiest, dirtiest, most patched-up uniform I had ever seen out of his bag and put it on.

Max's act began in the fourth inning and lasted until the seventh. A natural contortionist, Max would bend over in the coach's box like an ostrich with his head in the sand, trying to read the catcher's signals. Then he would break into a little jig to the old rock 'n roll hit, "Rock Around the Clock." At one point, he somehow managed to take a long gulp of water and then spray it out like a sperm whale for an interminably long period of time.

The fans loved his antics, especially when he started to mimic the mannerisms of the ballplayers and umpires as they took their place on the field.

Everybody was having a great time. There were smiles everywhere until Max came back to the bench at the end of each inning. As soon as he reached the dugout, out of sight of the audience, the glowing smile quickly left his face and was replaced with a look of agony. He started to groan and spit and I figured this couldn't be part of his act. I asked if he was all right and, rubbing his jaw in obvious pain, Max told me he had an abscess in a tooth and it was becoming infected.

I asked Max if there was anything I could do and he said he had to see a dentist, which I thought was a fairly appropriate response, but as soon as the half inning came to an end, Max sprinted out from his seat with a big grin on his face,

THOMAS DeFEO

there aren't enough funny things happening
minors, Max Patkin performs as a clown.

waving to the cheering crowd. This Pagliacci of baseball went the distance just like a champion, getting laughs on the field and commiseration in the dugout. Just like in the big leagues, the show must go on.

Miguel Dilone broke the Western Carolinas league base-stealing record tonight. His sixty-seventh stolen base broke a record that was set in 1970 and it came against Anderson here tonight.

George Cappuzzello was our pitcher and Dilone got on base his first time up. We knew he needed one steal to break the record, so there was no doubt he would try to steal at the first opportunity. There was a pretty good crowd at the game and they began cheering for Dilone to steal second.

Cappy stretched and then threw to first base. Dilone had broken for second and he had such a good jump that by the time the first baseman threw to second, Dilone had slid in safely.

Everybody went slightly bananas. Fireworks went off and Dilone was beaming with pride. Chuck Cottier, the manager of the Pirates, came out with a base that had been painted over in gold with "67" on it. The photographers and reporters came on the field and the game was held up as Cottier made the presentation to Dilone.

Finally, the umpire spoke up and told everybody, Cottier, Dilone, reporters and photographers, that it was not a stolen base. He had called a balk on Cappy and the base had been awarded to Dilone without the steal.

An announcement was made and the crowd booed. The photographers and reporters left the field and Cottier returned to the dugout, carrying the gold-painted souvenir base.

On the very next pitch, Dilone headed for third. This time there was an excellent throw by our catcher, Bob Wis-

WILFRID BINETTE

Visniewski was our regular catcher.

niewski, to Benny Hunt. It appeared we had Dilone, but the umpire didn't hesitate in calling him safe . . . and here came the cheers and the fireworks again, and Cottier, followed by the reporters and photographers, lugging that base once again.

Anderson, S.C.
July 21

Jack Walsh has turned into an enigma. After being highly touted early in the season as a potential superstar, Jack misplaced the whereabouts of the strike zone and the walks began to pile up. His lack of control eventually led to his demise. As one of the supposed mainstays of the pitching staff, Jack's failure to win was particularly disappointing to Len Okrie.

Jack was demoted from the starting rotation and banished to the Siberia of baseball, the bullpen. At first, nobody thought too much of it. Jack had to prove himself to get back in the starting rotation and we thought he would. As it turned out, our pitching got better all the time and Jack didn't get many chances to prove himself.

So, Jack got used to his new home in the pen and began to accept his fate. Everybody knew that someday soon he'd get his chance again; all he had to do was stay ready for it. But that day didn't come for quite some time. And his lack of control might not have been completely responsible.

First, you must understand Jack. Born and raised in Brooklyn, he is movie-star handsome. But he also has the brashness and accent of a hardened New Yorker. Jack is a big, solid guy, blessed with a good sense of humor. In fact, when he really gets going on something funny, he leans his head back, opens his mouth wide and out comes an incredibly loud and thunderous peal of laughter, which seems to escape from the depths of his being. It is one of the most authentic belly laughs I have ever heard and it echoes all over the ballpark.

We played tonight's game despite a downpour which left the field wet and slippery, especially in the outfield.

In the seventh inning, a Gastonia batter hit a low line drive to left field. Our left fielder was Kim Cates, a mountain of a guy who can hit some tremendous shots. Unfortunately, Kim is a much better first baseman than he is an outfielder. In fact, in the outfield, even a dry one, he looks like an elephant chasing a butterfly. So when he came rambling in to field this line drive, it was a potentially volatile situation.

Our bullpen is down the left-field line and naturally all of its occupants were watching as Kim slipped on the wet turf. After a lunge at the ball, he finally succumbed to the force of gravity and fell to the ground. He looked like a wild charging rhino that had been stopped in its tracks by a powerful shotgun blast.

The denizens of the bullpen broke into giggles and cackles, doing their best to suppress their laughter. Even Sheekey turned away to hide his reaction. It just isn't ethical in baseball to laugh at a teammate when a guy on the other team is racing around the bases, no matter how foolish your teammate looks.

But Jack, who had taken in the entire scene, just couldn't hold back. And there he was ho-hoing at the pratfall in the outfield.

Jack's laugh was so loud that it even was heard by Okrie, sitting way down in the dugout. Adhering stringently to the ethics of baseball, Len didn't see any humor whatsoever in Kim's spill and demanded to know of the guys in the dugout what was so darn funny about playing a single into a triple. Jack will have to suppress that laugh of his or he could have a change of address—from bullpen to doghouse.

Anderson, S.C.
July 28

OK, Jim Bouton, I read *Ball Four* and I learned about all those so-called "baseball Annies" who follow us pro baseball players around. In fact, it was a sociological phenomenon that I was looking forward to. Now that the season is more than half over, I'm still looking for a baseball Annie.

I heard the minor leaguer's life was a lonely one. Nobody told me it would be like joining the YMCA. I could probably join a local monastery in my spare time.

To put it bluntly, the social life in Anderson, as far as we A-Tigers are concerned, is nil, nonexistent, kaput!

I'll give you an example. Yesterday was Sunday and after the game, we had the night off and some of the guys decided to get together. What do you do on a night off? We put our heads together and decided to go big league and have a cookout, steaks, beer, the works.

About half the team showed up at Wiz and Jack's trailer, which is only a few hundred yards from my trailer, and Jack, who considers himself the next Galloping Gourmet, masterfully broiled our steaks on a makeshift grill. Along with the steaks, we had baked potatoes, salad and beer.

Everybody had a grand time, but after the eats were gone and everybody had enough beer, it was still quite early. This presented a problem, for we still wanted to go out, but since everything is closed on Sunday in South Carolina and nobody knew any girls, we were stymied.

Then somebody piped up and said, "Hey, why don't we go over to the local drive-in?"

That seemed like a good idea, so we all piled into our cars and made our way to the drive-in theater. As we arrived, we discovered to our amazement that the theater was sold out. I had never heard of a drive-in theater being sold out before.

Frustrated, but not thwarted, we checked the movie listings in the local paper. Tis started to read off the other shows playing in Anderson.

"Well, over at the Mall, they've got *Billy Jack,* but I guess everybody has seen that at least five times already . . . . Let's see, over at the Osteen *Paper Moon* is playing, but the last show started an hour ago . . . . Oh, yeah, there's one more, but you guys wouldn't be interested."

"What the hell is it?"

"The Sound of Music."

We looked at each other and shrugged. What choice did we have? And so fourteen professional ballplayers, looking for excitement, wound up watching *The Sound of Music* on their night off.

Anderson, S.C.
August 2

For the struggling hitter in baseball who is doomed to never be more than 30 percent efficient, at best, in his search for the almighty base hit, there comes a rare night, when, by a fluke, everything happens to fall into place and the ballplayer's faith is restored. I'm speaking of the perfect night, when a hitter has an equal number of hits per times at bat.

There's probably nothing quite so satisfying as a perfect night. Going back through Little League, high school, American Legion and college ball, I have never had a perfect night. I have had multi-hit games, but never a perfect game.

Tonight against the Spartanburg Phillies, my lifelong dream came true. In four at-bats, I walked, had two singles and a double. I also scored two runs and had two RBIs. A perfect 3–for–3.

What a warm, mellow glow comes to one's body on such a heavenly night.

Spartanburg, S.C.
August 9

I got razzed pretty good tonight by the Spartanburg Phillies for something I said about a week ago. I'm not much of a hot dog. I usually play it pretty straight and I don't often get razzed by other teams, but I must confess that I really deserved what I got on this occasion.

The last time we played Spartanburg, their broadcaster asked me to do a pre-game interview. Like the Greenwood Braves, the Phillies games are broadcast over a local station. Unlike Greenwood's irrepressible and zany Larry Gar, Spartanburg's broadcaster, Warner Fuselle, carries on a very straightforward interview.

After talking about some general baseball topics, Warner surprised me with a bit of data I wasn't really aware of—he asked me how come I hit the Phillie pitchers so hard, informing me that I was hitting .416 against them this season.

I was astounded. I knew I hit the Phillies well, but not at that incredible pace. What makes it more intriguing is that the Phillies have the best pitching staff in the league and, because of it, Spartanburg is firmly entrenched in first place for the second half of the season.

After giving some possible reasons for my success against the Phillies, Warner went on to discuss other matters, including my bit part in the film, *Love Story*.

He had found out, somehow, that I had been asked to appear in a scene in the picture based on the best-selling novel. Some of the film was shot on the Harvard campus while school was in session and one day a friend, a Harvard hockey player told me they were looking for students to appear in a scene taken at the hockey rink.

Naturally, I agreed to do it, especially when I learned would get paid. I got $5 and it cost me $2 to go see the movie when it came out. I was curious to see myself. If you saw the picture, maybe you noticed me. I was the left leg wearing a pair of jeans sitting in the arena watching the hockey game. That's all they showed of me, my left leg.

But Warner was very much interested in this and in th little bit of behind-the-scenes Hollywood I could tell him about. Like Ryan O'Neal cannot skate—the skating scene were actually taken with Bill Cleary, Harvard's hockey coach, playing O'Neal's part—and that most of the buildings in the movie are fictitious and that few "Cliffies" look like Ali McGraw and that even fewer Harvard hockey jocks go to Harvard Law School and graduate third in their class. I think I disappointed him with this information.

Finally, toward the end of the lengthy interview, I was feeling pretty pompous and smug, so when Warner asked me if I had any general impressions of the Phillies' team, I blurted out a parody on the famous line from *Love Story*.

"Well, Warner," I said, "what can I say. To me, playing Spartanburg means never having to say you're sorry . . ."

As soon as I said it, I regretted it. I prayed to heaven that nobody, especially the Phillie players, had heard that comment. But it was too late to take it back, so I just tried to forget all about it.

Tonight we played Spartanburg for the first time since the broadcast. We lost, 9–3, which was disappointing enough, but from a personal point of view, the evening was tragic.

They were throwing a pitcher I usually hit pretty well and I sort of figured I would maintain my .416 average. In the top of the eighth I came to bat for the fifth time and grounded out to the third baseman. That last at-bat completed my ohfer . . . to be specific, it gave me a big, fat 0–for–5. But my tragic performance was not yet complete, for as I jogged out to my position, I heard somebody call my name from the general direction of the Phillie bullpen. I turned around and as I did, I froze in horrible embarrassment, for the entire Spartanburg bullpen got up and gave a loud and raucous rendition of the theme from *Love Story* with some new, choice lyrics.

Charleston, S.C.
August 12

This could be a suicide note.

Remember how smoothly I was taking the season, just

coasting on my comfortable .275 batting average and thinking about next year's contract? Well, forget it. The bubble has burst, and the batting average is plummeting like the proverbial lead balloon. Alas, all I can hope for is the postponement of the rest of the season. Hopefully, I'll break my leg and won't have to play for the rest of the year. Here are the gory details:

Since August 2, I have encountered a disastrous slump, going 3–for–20 until today's doubleheader against Charleston. That sent the average down, down, down toward that stage of infamous mediocrity, .250. But I've got a tough, optimistic mind. All right, I said to myself, I'll just bang out three or four hits against the Pirates and get that average right back up into the .270s.

It was with that heroic and gallant attitude that I played the doubleheader. I felt good. I was quite confident of getting my share of hits. Then, on my first at-bat I hit a line shot to right, only to see the right fielder soak it up for an out. But, I rationalized, it was the hardest ball I had hit in over a week and it portended good things to come.

I tried using the same rationale on my second, third and fourth at-bats as I successively grounded out to short, flied out to center and grounded out to third. I was getting a little frustrated, but every ball I hit I stung pretty well. Don't worry, Rick, you'll get your hit, I promised myself.

When I popped up on my fifth at-bat and struck out on my sixth, the original doubting gloom came back to my mind. Now I was 0–for–6 on the day, but I could no longer rationalize my plate performances as I had on my previous unsuccessful at-bats. Now I was really getting burned, but being a pro, I put on a veneer of nonchalance that indicated that nothing was going to faze me, not even an 0–for–7.

On my seventh at-bat, I hit a one-hopper back to the Pirate pitcher, who took his time and easily threw me out at first. I stoically kept my countenance frozen in a trance of non-emotion, showing all my fans and teammates that even an 0–for–7 didn't bother me in the least. Yet I have to think I raised some suspicious looks from my teammates when in a fit of anger and frustration, I bit my bat so hard, it almost broke. I didn't show any emotion, though, while chomping on my Louisville Slugger.

But baseball is the perfect game and it takes care of its own. As it turned out, I came very, very close to changing a disastrous day into a triumphant victory. We were down, 2–1, going into the top of the seventh and somehow we loaded the bases with nobody out and guess who came to bat for the Tigers.

The adrenaline pumped through my tired body and my mathematical mind computed that the odds were in my favor to get a hit and be the hero. I guess the Charleston manager thought along the same lines for he called time out and brought in his top relief pitcher. Gee, I thought, what a nice compliment I had just been paid.

The new picher finished warming up and I stepped in to do battle and save my pride, and my sanity. The computer in my head was whirring away and an answer popped into my head. With the bases loaded and ahead by only one run, this guy is going to try very hard to throw a strike on his first pitch. I decided to swing at it, come hell or high water.

To my astonishment, here came the biggest, fattest, sweetest pitch I have ever seen, just begging me to knock the stuffing out of it. Obligingly, I swung.

It was one of those moments in your life you never forget. All of a sudden, there was the sharp, true, whack of wood against cowhide, the unmistakable sound and feel of a base hit. And then there was silence. It seemed to happen in slow motion . . . the ball leaving my bat, thrusting like a rocket leaving a launching pad, on a direct line toward the outfield. It was a simply beautiful sight as my mind began to visualize the headline: "Wolff Wins Game with Clutch Hit!"

Those were the thoughts in my mind as I saw out of the

corner of my eye the ball, my base hit, my only hit of the day, my game-winning, hero-making hit, going into the glove of the Pirate shortstop. The partisan crowd roared its approval of the play and, crushed, I slowly walked back to the bench. Our next batter hit into a double play and the game was over. We lost, 2–1, and my day was complete, a perfect 0–for–8.

Putting it all together in one day, I just narrowly missed being the hero and extended my hitting slump to a cataclysmic 3–for–28.

After you find my body and bury me, do me just one favor—please don't put my batting average on my tombstone.

Charleston, S.C.
August 13

There is nothing Brian Sheekey enjoys more than going into his sportscasting routine. He does a great hockey bit, spitting out the words in machine gun fashion, his voice packed with emotion, rising with the tempo of the game and the swell of the action. He seems to be driven by the roar of an invisible crowd.

At four o'clock this morning, Sheek made one of his great calls.

We were coming back from Charleston after the game and after driving for about two hours, the team decided to stop and eat. Bobby Kerr pulled into a truck stop on the road. It was a perfect setting for an episode of *Twilight Zone*, late at night in the middle of nowhere.

We all shuffled into the dining room and Sheek, Jack Walsh, Steve Tissot and I found a booth. After a brief perusal of the menu, Tis brought up a rather poignant observation. "Say gang, at four in the morning is it proper to order dinner or breakfast?"

It was a tough question. Jack scratched his chin and I just shrugged, but Sheek didn't have any problem. When the waitress came over, Sheek spoke right up.

"I'll have the 'Trucker's Special' with green salad, blue cheese dressing and a side order of pancakes with plenty of maple syrup."

An hour later, most of the team had finished and was boarding the bus. Our orders had still not arrived. We sat there, stomachs growling, when finally the waitress banged open the kitchen doors, perilously balancing our meals on her shoulder. Like Pavlovian dogs, we started to salivate, eagerly anticipating our long-awaited food. And then it happened. . . .

We saw it all so clearly. The waitress, concentrating on balancing the dishes, never saw the wet spot on the tiled floor. A tremendous clatter of smashing plates followed, salads tossed into the air like confetti, and pancakes flung like frisbees.

There was the waitress, pancakes strewn all over her shoulders and arms, bits of lettuce in her hair net, struggling to hold her position, one leg angled to the left, down on the other knee and the now empty tray still held aloft.

It was the perfect image for Sheekey's vivid imagination. As the scene unfolded and the waitress was performing her acrobatics, Sheek, undaunted by the fate of our meals, jumped out of his chair and bellowed, "Vadnais passes to Orr . . . Orr over to Esposito from the point . . . the slap shot . . . Giacomin, kick . . . save . . . a beauty!"

Gastonia, N.C.
August 16

This was our last visit of the season to Gastonia. I'm not too sad about the prospect of not returning.

It seems every time we've been here, they've had a new kind of torture waiting for us. This time the Rangers unveiled their latest weapon, a six-foot-six flamethrower who suffered from night blindness. To keep their pitcher from getting self-conscious as he groped in the darkness, the Ranger's stadium lights seemed dimmer than usual, so that everybody was enshrouded in darkness. That was very considerate of them.

95

The result was sheer torture. The Gastonia pitcher just wound up, reared back and fired, not necessarily knowing, or caring, where the ball went. All he cared about was that nobody could hit the ball, which we didn't. As they say, you can't hit what you can't see.

As I stepped into the batter's box for the first time, I peered out into the darkness and saw the vague silhouette of a monstrous pitcher. I could barely make out his arms and legs, so I knew I had no chance of seeing the pitch. I stepped out of the box and called time in order to ponder this situation. I glanced at the catcher, who seemed to be enjoying my predicament.

All I could do was prepare myself for the worst and say a little prayer. I had five chances at bat and I walked four times. On the other at-bat, I swung the bat, just for laughs, and I surprised myself by making contact. I lifted a nice, harmless fly ball to right field.

We eventually lost the game, 5–4, but the stats indicated what a strange game it was. We got two hits, both infield singles, and twelve of us struck out. Yet we got four runs, thanks to ten walks.

Greenwood, S.C.
August 18

I was sitting next to the window as our bus pulled up to a stoplight in downtown Greenwood. I had just awakened from a short snooze, which I am apt to do on bus rides, and it was with sleepy eyes that I peered out the window and quickly rubbed the sleep out of my eyes and looked again. I couldn't believe what I saw.

Down the street, coming our way, was a pickup truck equipped with four loudspeakers which were blaring something inaudible, and in the back of the truck were four figures, clad from head to toe in silvery white gowns and hoods. They were supporting a giant wooden cross. I thought to myself, "This can't be for real."

As the truck got closer, I could see the little scarlet red insignias on their gowns and the message from the loudspeaker became audible. A Ku Klux Klan rally was being held that night at the Greenwood Fairgrounds, right across from the Greenwood Braves' baseball field.

I was incredulous. I tried to figure it out rationally. I mean here it is, 1973, and I just saw four members of the KKK ride down Main Street wearing their white bedsheets and carrying a cross. Wait a minute. This has to be a joke . . . some sort of publicity stunt . . . an advertisement for a new movie, right? After all, this is the year nineteen hundred and seventy-three. I learned at school that the KKK went out of business back during the Depression. Come on, now, the KKK is defunct, dead, extinct. Isn't it?

The light eventually changed and our bus continued its way to the ballpark. I was stunned, but I had to get on with the game so I forgot about that little scene.

Later, around dusk, I was playing second base and Hal Underwood, my black teammate and double-play partner, was playing shortstop. All of a sudden, there was a distant, but distinctly loud roar of applause and we both turned around and looked over the right-field fence.

Off in the distance, the same cross which I had seen earlier that day was now engulfed in orange flames. A little off to the right there was a platform on which a figure in hood and gown was screaming into a microphone . . . "We got them damn niggers on the run and we got them damn Catholics running, too. . . ."

At that point I looked at Hal and he looked as incredulous as I did. He said nothing and the game resumed, but off in the background we could hear that hysterical voice.

There was no stopping us in the game. Cappy picked up his ninth win, Wisniewski had a three-run homer and I tripled, scored two runs and brought one home with a sacrifice fly. We won, 7–2.

Hal Underwood sparkled in the field and at bat. He made some fine plays in the field and at the plate he stroked two solid base hits and picked up another stolen base. He brought roars from he crowd and applause from his teammates and I kept wondering if the sound carried over to the Fairgrounds and hoping somebody would ask, "Who are they cheering for?"

Anderson, S.C.
August 22

"I hate those damn things; they are the worst things in the world," said pitcher Bob Shortell.

"I hope I never see another one as long as I live," declared Hal Underwood.

"They remind me of a book by Franz Kafka," commented Steve Tissot.

"Maybe I can train one to do some tricks and sell the act to a circus," mused Brian Sheekey.

What are these ballplayers taking about? Umpires? Drunken fans? Greasy hamburgers?

No, they are discussing the minor leaguer's constant companion, the cockroach.

It's getting toward the end of the year and everybody is getting a little grouchy. Little annoyances, once tolerated, are now explosive powder kegs, and one of the main bothers is the presence of those ubiquitous little brown cockroaches all over the clubhouse.

Earlier in the year, I had been very warm and open in my relationship with the little fellows. I considered them to be rather cute, twirling their brown antennae at me and running all around my locker. I let them nibble on my glove and shoes whenever they were hungry, allowed them to congregate in my undershirts and to lay their eggs and raise their young in the complete comfort of my warm-up jacket and, all in all, gave

98

them a free reign of my meager territory and belongings. Most of the other guys felt the same as I did and since we couldn't do much about them anyway, the team and the cockroaches just established a peaceful coexistence.

But as the weather continues to get hotter and as our loss column becomes larger, our tempers are getting shorter. All-out war has been declared on the roaches.

After writing my parents about the cockroach war, they sent me an article about cockroaches, describing their nature, biologically and otherwise. I underlined a few key passages and posted the article on the clubhouse wall. One of the underscored parts pointed out that cockroaches can metabolize just about everything and will eat just about anything.

I must say, the author's research was certainly accurate and thorough. A week or so after I posted the article, the cockroaches ate it.

Spartanburg, S.C.
August 26

There's about a week left in the season and some of the fellows who have had tough years are becoming slightly irritable. The feeling is not peculiar to Anderson's team. Tonight, for example, I witnessed the greatest exhibition of reaction to frustration I have ever seen.

Spartanburg's field is a beautiful place, and the stands look down onto the field. They are covered by a roof and a facade, approximately 100 feet from the field. In any case, it's a long drop from the roof to the playing field.

Bruce Butler, the Phillies' left-handed first baseman, was suffering through a rough night. Our pitcher, Bob Kaiser, who is particularly tough on left-handers, had fooled Butler badly on some curve balls and had struck him out three straight times. When Butler came to bat for his fourth time, the count went quickly to two strikes. Butler backed out of the box, thought about the inevitable, then stepped back in.

The 1973 Anderson Tigers: I'm third from the left, bottom row.

ANDERSON TIGERS

The third pitch was high, but Butler swung at it and missed for strike three. In a moment of utter frustration, Butler took his bat and, in one motion like a hammer thrower, flung it up, up and away, over the stands, over the facade, over the roof, over everything, and it disappeared into the darkness. Now, that's frustration!

Greenwood, S.C.
August 28

The season ended today and I had mixed emotions of relief and sadness. I was tired and looking forward to relaxing for a while before going back to school. But I wondered how long it would be before I missed Anderson and my Tiger teammates.

Cambridge, Mass.
September 22

I walked into the reference room in Lamont Library here and was browsing through back copies of *The New York Times* when I happened to spot a recent issue of *The Sporting News*. Naturally, it had been placed on a separate shelf so as not to violate the sacrosanct instruments of higher education. Here was my summer reading sustenance in a unique setting. I reached for it and found, not surprisingly, that it was covered with a fine layer of dust.

Here was the ballplayer's bible, the minor leaguer's Koran, and I, too, had been beckoned to partake of the insights and enlightenments that only *The Sporting News* could possess and bestow. My mind jumped to bus rides and locker rooms, to ball fields and hamburger joints. There I was again, facing the pitcher, gripping the bat, intent on every move.

I glanced around. No one had noticed what I was reading, yet it would be only a matter of time before I was discovered. I slipped the newspaper between B. F. Skinner's *Phylogeny and Ontogeny of Human Behavior* and R. F. Wittkower's *Architectural Principles of the Renaissance* and headed for a small quiet alcove far from the mainstream of traffic. There I uncovered my treasure and quickly turned to the minor league section and the Class A notes in particular. The familiar names, the teams, the towns were all there, but they seemed so far removed it was almost like entering a world of dreams, of fantasies.

Looking at the stats brought back a rush of memories—my weeks among the league leaders and that barren stretch in August when the fielders seemed to be standing everywhere I hit the ball. However, the .246 average was a respectable one for a rookie second baseman, the number of extra-base hits, runs scored and RBIs were encouraging signs, and that Western Carolinas record for participating in double plays was a pleasant recollection. All things considered, I felt that I had surmounted the first step of every amateur—proving he can do the job as a professional.

I was caught in this reverie between the past and the future when I noticed someone coming. I closed *The Sporting News,* returned the newspaper files and placed it back on the shelf. For the next few hours, sitting in the library, I was immersed in study.

Later, as I walked back to my dorm, a most perplexing question crossed my mind, which I don't think too many people here could answer: Is it more difficult to go into the hole behind second and throw a fast batter out at first, or to do a philosophical treatise on the use of pagan gods in Botticelli's "Study of Lucretia"?

Cambridge, Mass.
October 15

I've settled down to the life of a student, life in the Western Carolinas League buried deep in my past. I'm comfortably ensconced in my classes and in the dormitory apartment in Mather House that I share with four other students—all female.

The clubhouse in Anderson was nothing like this.

Actually, it's not what it seems and there is a story behind this arrangement.

When I left after what was to have been my senior year to pursue my baseball career, my friends and former roommates told me not to worry, they would take care of my accommodations for the following year. I should have realized they would try to pull off some kind of stunt.

Their idea of a joke was to room me with four Cliffies—students at Radcliffe.

When I arrived, they were sitting around watching the Bobby Riggs-Billie Jean King tennis match. After recovering from the initial shock, we decided to set down some ground rules. Since we were going to be living together in this unique set-up, certain rules and regulations were necessary.

We have a five-room suite with five separate bedrooms, so there is no problem there. But we share a common hallway and bathroom.

The first thing we had to do was determine what would be the proper dress during hours of relaxation. My main concern was that they would be constantly chattering on the phone or always in the bathroom, which would be strewn with dozens of pantyhose.

Their concern was that, as a professional athlete, I would be drinking beer constantly and have all-night orgies.

So, I called this "clubhouse meeting" and we set down guidelines. Certain trivialities had to be ironed out. Since I was in the minority, whenever I wanted to use the john, I had to signify by closing the door that it was in use. They were permitted to leave the door open, but if I was headed toward the john, I was obliged to forewarn them by shouting I was on my way.

I also was expected to wear a robe around the place and to maintain a certain amount of quiet if I wanted to sit around drinking beer and watching the Monday-night football game. And I was not to leave beer cans lying around.

I was also warned that every day at four, they would have their brandy or tea, which I came to realize, was the Radcliffe version of a Kaffee Klatch.

When I told my friends about my roommates, they kind of got this ribald leer in their eyes. But there is nothing like that at all. It as an unusual arrangement and I'm not so sure their boy friends are too crazy about the fact that after they say good night to the girls, I'm left there with them. But this expanded version of the Odd Couple is a very interesting experience.

I have come to look upon Vicki, Ellen, Mary and Linda like a big brother looking after four younger sisters. Our relationship is purely platonic. Even my dad thinks of them as his four daughters and on business trips to Boston, if I'm unable to get together with him, he takes the girls to dinner.

It is a great change of pace living with the girls and we have an excellent relationship. They are four brilliant ladies, two English majors and two art majors, and we have many stimulating discussions. It is all quite different for me, especially after spending an entire spring and summer in the constant company of young men.

As time goes on, the girls and I have become very close. I've taught them to drink beer and they've taught me to drink tea and brandy.

There is one thing, however, that I can never get used to, and that is walking into the bathroom and always finding the seat down.

Cambridge, Mass.
December 3

I've heard that the Detroit Tigers have decided to cut down on their minor league teams and have relinquished their Anderson franchise.

As I understand the logistics of the minor league situation, this is going to mean the Tigers will have their usual amount of incoming ballplayers, new draftees and free agents, plus the holdovers. But now, with an entire twenty-five-man roster for a minor league team completely disbanded, this is going to mean there will have to be an extra twenty-five ballplayers released, for there will be fewer places for them.

So, knowing that I played in Anderson, and although I thought I had a pretty good year, until I get my contract I will be a little concerned as to what plans, if any, the Tigers have for me. The next two months the waiting will be difficult.

Has my professional baseball career come to an abrupt end without fanfare, without a "Rick Wolff Night," at which the Anderson Tigers permanently retire my number 6?

1974

Cambridge, Mass.
January 16

My anxiety and apprehension ended today. I received my contract from the Tigers. They really do want me and need me, after all. It's a Clinton contract calling for a salary of $550 a month, an increase of $50 a month over last year. I decided to give some thought as to how I might get more money.

Cambridge, Mass.
January 27

I returned my unsigned contract to Clinton, just like the big holdouts do. I enclosed a cordial letter to Fritz Colschen, the Clinton general manager, explaining that I was looking forward to playing in Clinton, but I felt my record last year should entitle me to a pay boost of $5 a day, an additional $150, which would give me $650 a month.

Apparently, my pleas were understood and my argument was sound because I received a new contract from Clinton. It called for a compromise figure of $600 a month (a raise of $3.33 a day). There was also a note from Fritz Colschen saying he had taken the matter up with Hoot Evers, Director of Player Development, and that I had been granted an additional $50 from the previous contract. I signed it and returned it.

"Shoot, man, look who's back for more."

I turned around as I heard the familiar Texas drawl. It was my old buddy, Benny Hunt, still wearing his stylish black cowboy boots and long black sideburns, and with a toothpick sticking out of the side of his mouth. Just like last summer. He hasn't changed a bit.

Before I could say anything to Ben, the hallway door opened and out strolled none other than the Sheek, Brian Sheekey, all slicked up and ready to go on the town. He was twenty pounds heavier than last year.

"Hey, hey, Wolffie, how ya doing? Gee, you're looking good. I lost about thirty pounds myself over the winter. Got to stay in shape, you know."

Good old Sheek. Hasn't lost his touch. Still the best con man in Tigertown.

Two other teammates from Anderson walked into the lobby. I recognized Wiz right away, and he called me Wolffman as he did all last summer. The other seemed to know me, but I couldn't place him until I got a little closer. Finally, I recognized Dan Kaupla, but the long flowing locks which distinguished him last year were gone.

"Kaup, what happened to your hair?"

"Well, Rick, I didn't have too good a year last season, so I figured I'd better keep all the coaches happy and off my back around here by getting my hair cut nice and short."

I chatted with these two characters for a few minutes, then got my room key and dragged my stuff up to my room. There I found three beds just like last year and as I unpacked, I prayed that the other two guys neither smoked nor snored.

I had no sooner taken off my jacket and tie when George Hart, another ballplayer from Anderson days, walked into the room, greeted me and asked me if I wanted to enroll in the Fetzer Hall Championship Table-Top Hockey Tournament.

"Gee, George, I just got here a few minutes ago. Let me get settled and I'll speak to you later about playing hockey."

I couldn't help wondering if hockey players in training camp kill time by playing baseball games at night.

Finally, I unpacked and my two roomies walked in. One I knew, Jack Larkin, a pitcher who had played for Orangeburg last year. It was a co-op team and he had been optioned there by the Tigers. He was a good guy and I looked forward to trading old Western Carolinas stories with him.

The other fellow was Tom Thompson, a shortstop who had played in the Rookie League last year. He's a graduate of Oral Roberts University and also seems like a nice guy.

They were both surprised by my question about whether they smoke or snore, but they both said no. I guess we'll get along fine.

I took a stroll around camp, trying to reacquaint myself with the surroundings. I looked around and I noticed something odd about Tigertown. It hadn't changed one bit, it was exactly the same as last year.

I began to think about that and realized that it would probably be the same next year, too, for spring training is a timeless concept. Time is an enemy to professional athletes and if all the facilities look the same from year to year, we can trick ourselves into believing that we're not changing either, not getting any older.

The more I thought about it, the more I realized it was true. Guys here don't worry about the energy crisis, the impeachment, the war in the Middle East. All they worry about is their batting average, what movie is playing at the local drive-in and where they can get a date for Friday night.

Tigertown really is a fantasy land where time has no meaning.

Lakeland, Fla.
March 6

It's hard to believe, but I just finished my first day of spring training in my second year of professional ball. It was exactly the same as last year's, except that now I'm a veteran and I know my way around.

The routine was familiar. Up at 8:00, breakfast, and ready to go to work on the field at 9:30 sharp. The old wooden clubhouse was jam-packed with ballplayers and the ol' familiar fragrance of spring training was everywhere . . . sun lotion, tobacco chew and pine tar.

It seems more crowded here than last year, which is odd considering they have one less team to fill. In fact, they have about 150 guys in camp with only about eighty-five jobs available, so this year many ballplayers will be released or optioned out. As for me, I've been placed on a Lakeland roster, but I know from past experiences that it's much too early to consider anything definite.

I lined up with the rest of the guys and received my working clothes. This year, I'm happy to report, I've been assigned number 44, a reasonable number for a second baseman (Hank Aaron started out at that position). I dropped 45 digits in a year, a sign of newfound status.

I saw all my old buddies from Anderson—or most of

them, at least—Al Newsome, Jeff Natchez, George Cappuzzello, Hal Underwood, Luis Atilano. It was like a big reunion, but I began to realize that some of my old teammates didn't make it through the winter.

I went up to Steve Litras, who with his newly grown mustache looks more like Groucho Marx than ever, and after talking about the Knicks and Rangers, I asked him about Jack Walsh.

Steve paused for a second, lowered his head and said, simply, "Jack was released a few days before Christmas. A tough time to get it. He's selling insurance down here in Lakeland. He got married, you know."

"I know," I said. "Maybe he'll come by to watch a practice."

"I doubt it," Steve said, shaking his head. "I don't think Jack will ever come around again."

I felt a big paw clamp down on my shoulder and a voice from behind me boomed out, "Wolffie, how ya doing?"

It had to be Bob Shortell. I turned around and, sure enough, I was greeted by a warm smile and Shorty's suntanned face.

"Hey, hey, Shorty, it's good to see you. Tell me, have you torn down any steel doors lately?"

Shorty had a propensity last year in Anderson to tear down the steel clubhouse door whenever he pitched and lost. Luckily for the owners and us, Shorty won more than he lost.

We chatted for a while and I asked him if he had seen Steve Tissot. He told me Tis was now playing with a rock band in Delaware.

"Hey, Shorty, I saw Nat Calamis while I was at school this past fall. He's working for a radio station in Providence, married and he seems to be very happy."

"That's what I've heard, Rick. Let me tell you, Nat really missed his girl and was getting anxious to settle down. He played hard, but you know you've got to be a little whacky over baseball to keep the spark alive."

Just then, the unmistakable deep voice of Ed Katalinas came roaring over the PA system.

"Good morning, gentlemen . . . it's a beautiful morning to play baseball here in Tigertown. . . ."

All 150 uniformed potential big leaguers started to trot out on the field for calisthenics and the beginning of another spring training, a new year.

Here we go again!

Lakeland, Fla.
March 11

Each spring training has a new pheenom. This year, it's an outfielder named Ron Le Flore.

Ron rooms next door to us on the second floor. He's built like the proverbial brick outhouse and looks like he should be playing for the Detroit Lions, not Tigers.

Not only is he strong, he can run. I got my first look at his speed today in an intra-squad game. Ron hit a routine one-hopper to the shortstop. I was sitting on the bench at the time when Duke McGuire, a first baseman who was familiar with Le Flore's ability, nudged me and said, "Watch this."

Ron was chugging down the first-base line and the shortstop easily fielded the grounder, lined up his throw, took his little crow hop and threw a solid shot to the first baseman. Ordinarily, on a ball like that, the runner should be out by four or five steps. I watched the flight of the ball to first and my mouth dropped. Le Flore was about ten feet past the bag when the ball reached the first baseman.

The ball was hit hard, almost a seed right at the shortstop, who played it flawlessly and made a good throw. Ron must weigh 195 pounds and he's a right-handed batter. How could he be safe by so much?

When he came up for his next-at-bat, a little group of curiosity seekers had gathered. This time he walked, but stole second and third, and didn't even slide although the catcher got off some good throws. This was becoming hard to believe.

110

On his third at-bat, a bigger crowd had assembled. This time he stroked a clean single right to the center fielder. The outfielder took it on one hop and fired it into second. By the time the ball got there, Le Flore was standing on second, not even breathing hard. It was evident that this guy could run, had power and hustled, a bona fide major league prospect, almost can't-miss material.

It will be a great story if Ron makes it. You'll have to admit he's done it the hard way. He was scouted in prison by Billy Martin, who had heard some glowing reports about the young man. Ron is on probationary parole, serving time for armed robbery, and baseball is his ticket to freedom and to a happy, useful life. You can't help rooting for a guy like that.

Lakeland, Fla.
March 14

Hal Underwood is gone from camp. I haven't heard if he just left or if he was released.

That's twenty ballplayers from last year's Anderson team who will not be playing in the Detroit organization this year.

Hal had a good year at Anderson, offensively. He hit close to .290, led the league in triples and had about forty stolen bases. His problem was defense. Hal made an unbelievable number of errors at shortstop. Many seemed to be errors of carelessness or pressure more than anything else. He'd make a great play and then throw a light beam toward the right-field seats.

Yet we all felt Hal had the tools to move up. He was impatient to make good. Every so often when Hal felt he was slipping from his self-imposed timetable and when the taunts of a few fans started to get to him, he talked about quitting and going back home to Detroit. He'd talk it out with me or some other guys and we'd convince him to stick it out. Hal felt certain that if he had a good year in Anderson, he'd move right up to Montgomery or Evansville. He was counting on it.

Things were going smoothly this spring until last week. He was the shortstop for Montgomery and hitting well. Even his fielding had improved considerably. But then, apparently, the roof caved in. The AA team lost some games and I heard that Hal was responsible for some of the losses because of some throwing errors. A week later, he wasn't even playing in spring training. I knew he wouldn't take to sitting on the bench and, sure enough, he left camp.

Lakeland, Fla.
March 16

I'm in the process of wasting one entire day of my life.

I'm fully aware that one is only allowed a finite number of days on God's earth and that it's a sin to waste an entire day. Today, however, is developing very seriously into a waste, a total waste.

You see, it's raining in Tigertown and there is absolutely nothing to do. Simply nothing.

Here's a rundown of my day's activities. I got up at approximately 8:00 A.M., looked out the window, saw that it was drizzling and got dressed. I ate breakfast, went down to the clubhouse and sat around doing nothing for about an hour. Finally, at 10:00, we were told practice was off and we were dismissed for the day.

I returned to my room, lay down on my bed. I stared at the ceiling for a while, trying to figure out what I should do with my free time. At 11:00, I tried writing a letter. After a few fruitless attempts, I gave up. I had nothing important to write about.

At 11:30, I got out my cassette recorder and listened to some music.

At 12:00, I went down to the cafeteria, grabbed a sandwich and iced tea for lunch.

From 1:00 to 4:00, I stayed in my room and tried to sleep. I couldn't, so I stared at the ceiling some more.

At 4:00, I went out and watched *Mission Impossible* on television. I had seen this particular episode several times and knew how it ended, but I sat through it anyway.

At 5:00, I went back to the cafeteria and ate dinner. Salisbury steak and potatoes. No gravy.

At 6:00, I watched the news on television. I finally fell asleep and woke up just as Harry Reasoner was giving tonight's comment.

At 7:00, I tried to write a letter, but couldn't. So I stared at the ceiling again.

Did you know that in room 222 in Fetzer Hall in Tigertown, Lakeland, Florida, there are exactly 4,892 holes in the perforated ceiling?

Lakeland, Fla.
March 19

Tonight's the night and all of Tigertown is excited.

No, they're not releasing anybody. Tonight is the big Championship Table-Top Hockey game between veteran outfielder Bob (Mollie) Molinaro and the reigning champ—you guessed it—Brian (the Sheek) Sheekey.

The whole affair was built up and publicized to the hilt, just as though it were the final game of the Stanley Cup playoffs. Game time was announced over the Tigertown public address system by Montgomery manager, Jim Leyland.

Right after dinner, some of the organizers started to block off entrances to the main floor lounge of Fetzer Hall, and they got Al Newsome and Bob Wisniewski, two of the biggest and strongest guys in camp, to act as ticket takers and bouncers. Admission to the game was fifteen cents. Scalpers were getting considerably more.

By 6:20, a sizeable crowd had gathered inside the lounge while the game, a hand-manipulated device with plastic players

113

on pencil-thin poles and a wooden chip for a puck, was brought down and placed on the center table. Outside the lounge doors, some hustlers were taking bets on the match. The inside word had Sheekey as the favorite for, as one insider put it, "Nobody, but nobody, beats the Sheek when it counts."

At 6:30 sharp, the lounge was packed to the ceiling— guys standing on chairs and crowding one another for a better view. Then the two contestants arrived; first, Bob Molinaro, who was backed by his two trainer-managers, Brian Lambe and Jim Nettles. Both wore white T-shirts with "Kid Mollie" inked on their backs. They led the cheers for Mollie and were confident that the Sheek could be taken.

Mollie arrived in fighting apparel, sneakers, gym shorts, no shirt, wearing a bathrobe with his hands wrapped in towels. He jumped up and down to demonstrate his fitness and his eagerness for battle.

The older players in the crowd heartily applauded his entrance and instantly began to chant, "Go Mollie, go . . . go, Mollie . . . go."

The place was quickly rising to a frenzy, everybody yelling and screaming. It was really something else.

Then the Sheek arrived supported by his followers. They pushed through the crowd to the main table and Sheek's fans gave him a rousing reception. It was just like a heavyweight championship fight with people going nuts at the sight of their favorite.

Sheek had not dressed out of the ordinary for the occasion and he stood glaring at Mollie, who had dared to upstage him with his boxing attire.

Finally, George Hart, the main organizer, promoter and entrepreneur, set down the ground rules. There were to be three periods of five minutes each, timed by a clock especially purchased for this game. The Sheek and Mollie shook hands and they went to it. The puck was dropped at center ice.

It was soon apparent that Sheekey had more expertise at

maneuvering his little cardboard hockey men and that Mollie was just trying to stay close. I knew that somehow, somewhere, the Sheek would come through in this crucial game; he was center stage, just the way he likes it, and I was positive he wouldn't let this opportunity slip away.

As the game progressed I began to see new developments and I was having my doubts. The first period was scoreless, as Sheek relentlessly pounded Mollie's goal with a torrent of shots, but Mollie defended himself well. The second period was much the same, as Mollie kept fending off Sheek's shots. I could see the frustration mount on Sheekey's face.

Then, out of nowhere, Mollie got off a pretty good shot that somehow rolled into Sheekey's goal. The crowd was stunned, but then erupted into an overwhelming ovation for Mollie.

An upset was in the making. Sheek was distraught at this response for his opponent. The king could not abide deserters. He was determined to retrieve his following. With renewed vigor, Sheek came roaring back. He pummeled Mollie with shots, but to no avail. The second period ended, 1–0, in favor of Molinaro.

The third period saw the Sheek fight for his life. Mollie took up the offensive and began to charge the Sheek's goal. Brian had no choice but to stop the shots, realizing that he couldn't score while on the defense. Precious seconds ticked away and the crowd began to recognize the Sheek's futile position. They began to urge Mollie on, pushing him to score more goals, to make it a rout. They had the ol' Sheek on the ropes.

"Two minutes to go in the game," shouted the timer.

Now almost everybody had sided with Molinaro, exhorting him to beat the cocky Sheek. But the Sheek wasn't dead yet. He moved quickly, with a deft pass here and a flashy shot there, and, bingo, the Sheek was on the scoreboard.

Suddenly, there was silence. Now the score was 1–1 with

about a minute to play in regulation time and everybody was wondering if an overtime period was to be played and if so, how long it would be. It was naturally assumed by all that the game would go into overtime. Everybody, that is, except the Sheek.

The crowd began to count down the seconds of regulation time. Ten . . . nine . . . eight . . . Everybody was still asking about overtime and arguing about how long it should be; in fact, some weren't paying attention to the action as the seconds ticked off . . . three . . . two . . . one . . .

Then the Sheek—almighty and powerful—omniscient and never-to-be-forgotten Sheek—blasted home the winning goal just as the timer ticked off the final second.

The crowd went wild. Sheekey had won it, 2–1, a classic duel in a classic hockey game, won in the most dramatic fashion imaginable.

Sheek threw up both arms in triumph, aglow with his victory, his round face smiling like a Cheshire cat, accepting congratulations and adulation from all. The crowd was his.

The Sheek had struck again.

Lakeland, Fla.
March 24

The ax falls swiftly here in Tigertown.

Today it fell for the first time, chopping off the dreams of fifteen minor league ballplayers, and the bad news spread through Fetzer Hall like wildfire.

At 8:15 this morning Jack Larkin, one of my roommates, announced to Tom Thompson and me, "The first cuts are up."

We sprinted down the hall to the bulletin board where the bad news was posted. Already there was a crowd of guys gathered around the fatal sheet of paper.

There it was, in the cold black and white of the typed page:

116

"The following are to report to Mr. Evers' office this morning at nine o'clock sharp: Robert Perkins, Gregory Kuhl, Patrick Grant, George Hart, Ronald Hargett, Daniel Kaupla, Benjamin Tensing, Brian Sheekey . . ."

Brian Sheekey? I couldn't believe it. I was stunned. I took a closer look. Sure enough, there was the list, including the name Brian Sheekey. He had been released. Upon closer inspection, I noticed that the vast majority of guys who were cut had been in Anderson last summer.

But the Sheek? Cut? That's hard to comprehend, especially so early in the morning. I mean, the Sheek was a bit paunchy and had some bad luck last year, but, gee, he was still a pretty good pitcher, and he even threw a no-hitter last year against Orangeburg.

I walked back to my room, speechless. The Sheek. How was it possible? Sheek walked through life with an invisible shield protecting him from the fates that haunt the average minor leaguer. Sheek was the man bathed in the spotlight, the storyteller, the man on center stage, impervious to everything around him, exuding confidence and assurance, the life of the party. Him cut? I still couldn't believe it.

I had to walk by Sheek's room to get to mine. I peeked in his door. The lights were off, but Sheek's two roomies had gotten up to see the list. The Sheek, good ol' Sheek, was still in bed, his clothes strewn all over the place, and it was quite obvious that he wouldn't be awake until 9:30, at least, a half hour past his appointment with Hoot Evers.

Typically, the Sheek would be late for his own release, sort of like missing your own funeral.

I returned to my room and stretched out on my bed. I had a sudden thought. Knowing the Sheek, I expected he would be back on the practice field later that morning. Somehow, he would convince Hoot that he still hasn't lost his touch, that his slider is just coming into true form, that he'll still be a big leaguer, and that he deserves another chance. I convinced myself that I would see the Sheek's rotund body come bouncing out for practice that morning.

It's 5:00 P.M. now. I didn't see the Sheek out on the practice field today and as I went by his room, I took another peek. His bed was made, his clothes and bags were gone.

I went out on my way to the cafeteria and there was the Sheek in the lobby, with his bags, waiting for a taxi to pick him up and take him to the airport. I felt very sad.

I waited with him until the taxi arrived and when it did, I started to say good-bye, but the words wouldn't come.

Finally, I blurted out, "Sheek, I don't think any of us will ever forget you. . . You have . . . charisma."

"Gee, Rick," he replied, "maybe I ought to see a doctor about it."

Lakeland, Fla.
March 25

Once the cuts start coming around here and guys start to leave in bunches, Fetzer Hall becomes a little spooky.

The ghost of the cuts begins to rise from the halls of the third floor, where most of the rookies are, and once it gains momentum, it strikes down into the second floor, down by all the safe and sound veterans. It manifests itself in many ways, which has been especially evident this spring.

Tonight, around 9:30, I was watching television in the second-floor lounge with about six other guys when the noise started. It came from the floor directly above us, and it was hardly noticeable at first. But the ghost was on the rampage.

"Hey, turn down the TV, something's going on upstairs," one of the alarmed first-year men said.

The older players, the ones who have been through a couple of spring trainings, didn't even pay the noise any attention. By now the noise upstairs was loud and distinct. The sound of crashing furniture and metal frames was unmistakable.

118

"What the hell is going on up there?" the same rookie asked again. "Don't you guys hear that?"

Another crash.

"Shut up, rook," said one of the veteran pitchers. "It's just The Exorcist upstairs."

Everybody laughed except the rookie. Nervous and fidgeting, he sat back in his chair and looked up at the ceiling. Now there was a low moaning mixed in with the thumping and smashing sounds.

"Dammit, somebody's hurt upstairs," the rookie said, and with that he jumped out of his chair and raced up the stairs to see what was going on. Nobody else in the lounge moved.

A few minutes later, the rook came back into the lounge. He looked pale, as though he had seen a ghost. I turned to him and asked, "What did you see?"

"You wouldn't believe it," he said. "Some guy was up there going crazy. He had a bat and he was smashing the walls and the furniture and the floor and he was crying about going home to his parents and . . ."

"Was it the big first baseman?" I asked.

"Yeah, yeah, I think it was."

"He got released today," I explained. "He was a pro ballplayer from March 5 to March 25, a total of twenty days. Wouldn't you cry, too?"

Lakeland, Fla.
April 4

When practice was over today, most of the guys rushed to the television set to watch the first game of the major league season.

Ordinarily, minor leaguers don't get very involved in what's going on in the bigs. But this was a special day. The Braves were playing the Reds on television and Hank Aaron needed one home run for No. 714, which would tie Babe Ruth.

There were about twenty guys watching and Aaron came up in the first inning with two on and hit his home run. Just like that. I mean it looked that easy.

We were all professionals and we just sat there, in silence, awestruck. It was almost an anticlimax. Like there should have been more drama, a drum roll or something. He just made it look so easy.

How can a guy just go up there, with all that pressure, with the whole world watching and waiting, how can he just go up and swing the bat and hit a home run? It was incredible.

Lakeland, Fla.
April 10

Jack, Tom and I were having our usual bull session tonight about roster changes and the inevitable cuts. It became ominously clear that many of the ballplayers from last year's Anderson team have been released.

The three of us began to recapitulate the casualties from the 1973 Anderson Tigers, a team that finished last in the Western Carolinas League. Believe it or not, we counted up to twenty guys who haven't survived.

We reasoned that only guys with top-notch seasons in Anderson last year would get another chance at playing this summer.

Early this morning the ax fell again. Among those who were whisked away was Bob (Shorty) Shortell. Fetzer Hall rocked with a new wave of mass paranoia, especially for us Anderson survivors. Shorty had a great year at Anderson. He was 8–5 and his earned-run average was under three, which isn't bad when you're pitching for a last-place team.

The way they let you know you've been cut around here is weird. It's 1984—Newspeak—over the ubiquitous PA system. At any time of day or evening, the PA may be interrupted of its syrupy music and the familiar, gruff voice of Hoot Evers comes across with that chilling message:

"The following ballplayers are to report to Mr. Evers' office . . ."

Everybody stops what he is doing. Radios are clicked off, stereos turned down, showers turned off, toilets stop flushing and everybody holds his breath. You can hear a pin drop as everybody listens intently, hoping not to hear his name, for you can be certain if Hoot mentions your name, he isn't calling it to give you a raise. You're going to get a plane ticket . . . one way.

As soon as he finishes reading the names, sacrificing another fifteen or twenty bodies to the almighty baseball god, the music begins and you can hear one gigantic collective sigh of relief from the survivors.

Spring training is a daily battle of survival and as the time goes on, the tension mounts.

As the final cuts approach, the sickness becomes almost intolerable. You can give a guy a nervous breakdown by saying, "Hey, I saw Hoot's clipboard today and he had your name crossed out."

I'll give you an example of the hysteria that can set in. Yesterday, there were rumors that today would be another day of axing. Everybody was expecting about a dozen or so guys to be cut and only the high-priced bonus babies went to bed and enjoyed a restful night.

Tom, Jack and I went to bed around midnight. We hadn't said much before turning in. Jack was worried. In his last outing, he didn't look very sharp and all three of us had the same thought—this might be Jack's last night in Tigertown.

As a result, Jack didn't sleep a wink all night. He kept tossing and turning all night and he got up six times during the night to see if the roster had been posted, as if it was being delivered by Santa Claus when all the little kiddies were fast asleep.

I felt sorry for Jack, but my patience was growing short when he announced at 6:30 in the morning that the roster still hadn't been posted. Tom and I told him to shut up and go back to sleep, but Jack couldn't. Here's his itinerary for the rest of the morning:

6:45—Jack gets up again, goes down the hall, comes back and announces the roster hasn't been posted yet. We curse.

7:00—Jack doesn't feel well. He can't sleep. He gets up, knocking over a chair, and goes for some aspirin. He stubs his toe and yells, waking us up again. We curse.

7:15—Jack is certain he hears somebody in the hall. He hops out of bed. A minute later he comes back. It was only the night watchman. Still no roster. We curse.

7:30—Jack decides he can't sleep, he's too nervous. To calm himself, he puts on the radio, waking us up again. We curse and threaten violence.

8:00—Tom and I get up for breakfast, neither of us feeling very well. We haven't slept much. Jack is fast asleep. Tom and I go down the hall. The roster is posted. Jack's name is on the Clinton squad. He still has a job. Tom and I talk about going back and waking him up, but we decide he's suffered enough already.

Clinton, Iowa
April 16

I survived the cuts and I'm on my way to a new season in a new part of the country—Clinton, Iowa.

Like the Navy, where one can see the world, pro baseball is exciting in that one can see the country. I really can't wait to embrace the heartland of America, the cornfields of Iowa.

The plane flight from Tampa to Chicago was a vast improvement over last year. No more knuckleball flights to Anderson. This flight was strictly big league, good food, pretty stewardesses, current magazines.

On the plane, I tried to formulate an impression of the Midwest before I got there. I came up with two extreme ac counts. One was from last year, when a bunch of the guys went to see the movie *Paper Moon,* which takes place in Kansas or Iowa. During one scene, which shows a flat and dusty wide open field, Mike Corbett, an outfielder who had played at Clinton, said "You guys see how flat and dusty that place is? Well, that's exactly what Clinton is like."

I quickly rid my mind of that impression and recalled some scenes from the television show *Apple's Way,* which takes place in a town called Appleton, Iowa. On the show, life is beautiful and pleasant with green grassy knolls, rolling hills, fresh fruit and corn, balmy temperatures and a carefree attitude that pervades the entire existence of the native Iowan.

Iowa must be heaven on earth, a true nirvana for all us smog-choked, bleary-eyed New Yorkers. If *Apple's Way* is even halfway accurate, I may renounce all my eastern ties and settle down in Appleton.

In any event, I'm excited. It's the start of a new season, with new people, on a new team, in a new league, and with the promise of visiting such exotic places as Wisconsin Rapids, Wisconsin, Danville, Illinois, and Burlington, Iowa.

In Chicago, we were met by a small welcoming committee. We boarded the team bus and drove due west, approximately two and a half hours, right into the town of Clinton.

The town is located on the banks of the Mississippi River and I must admit, I was a little disappointed at my first look at the great river.

Clinton is a river town, lying right on (and sometimes in) the Ol' Miss. Being a die-hard romantic, I was exhilarated as we approached the famed river, which separates the east and west of the United States. Just think, a beautiful, shimmering river, known for its elegant showboats and Mark Twain; the true gateway to the heartland of our country.

I was a bit miffed at seeing we had to pay a toll to go over this grandiose body of water, but my spirits were dampened even more as I looked down. The great Mississippi appeared to me to be just another muddy brown river. It wasn't sparkling clean, with the sun beaming down on it. It was just another dumpy, polluted river. Large, but dumpy.

We crossed a gigantic span bridge and had our first view of Clinton, Iowa. It was just the beginning of spring and there weren't any trees in bloom and looking down from the bridge on to the muddy waters of the river, we could see almost all of Clinton.

Down the way, maybe a mile from the bridge, we could see a huge municipal park and a few light standards. Obviously, that was the Clinton ballpark. It was next to the river, the outfield fence no more than 100 yards from the banks.

We pulled into the motel where we would be staying for the next three days and the first thing we did was grab the local paper and begin looking for a place to stay for the next six months. It's not as easy as it sounds because not everybody likes to rent to ballplayers.

Four of us spotted something that sounded good and we made a call. The lady invited us to go over and look at the place.

We hopped a bus and headed for the apartment, which was on the other side of town and that gave us a good chance to look over the town. The bus traveled right up Main Street.

Clinton has an elongated shape, meaning it spreads out along the banks for several miles, but it doesn't go very far inland. You can walk for miles and miles from north to south but you can only walk a couple of miles from east to west.

Clinton is a nice town. There's one main drag where all the banks, office buildings and the big stores are, and there are a lot of railroad tracks all over the place.

In the exact center of town is the biggest building, the courthouse, an old brick edifice with a little cannon up front and the town clock and the bells go off every hour on the hour informing the whole town of the exact time. It's very rustic and quaint.

124

CLINTON HERALD

This is Clinton, Iowa, and if the Mississippi River
overflows, Riverview Stadium will be knee-deep.

Right across from the courthouse are some railroad tracks and right across the railroad tracks is the home of the Clinton Pilots—Riverview Stadium—right there smack in the middle of town.

The ballpark was built in the thirties, I'd say. It's not exactly run-down, but it's not the most modern thing in the world. The infield is nicely kept and the outfield is fine, and there's an iron rod fence around the outfield and a scoreboard straight away in center field. They say the water drains pretty well here and it seems to be a good place to have a home ballpark and a nice place to stay for the next six months.

At first impression, Clinton is a pleasant town, clean and unhurried, and the buildings are old. It's not a growing town—the population is about 30,000. The people here seem friendly, very anxious to speak to you and you get the impression if you walk down Main Street and you're a ballplayer, you sort of stick out and the people know who you are because you look so different from everybody else.

The main industry of Clinton, besides farming, is a gigantic corn-processing company. There's also a huge Mr. Planter's Peanuts silo in town. In the early morning, occasionally, if the wind is blowing the wrong way, one can get a pretty heady whiff from these factories, between the sweet burning of corn and the crushing of peanuts to make peanut oil. On hot days, they say, all you have to do is walk outside and you smell like a peanut butter sandwich.

I think I'll like it here. It's very chilly now, there aren't many leaves on the trees yet and it's really not conducive to good baseball. But it does hold the promise of a good summer of baseball.

I somehow got hooked up with Jeff Natchez and we had agreed to team up as roommates and look for an apartment to share. Jeff played at Anderson last year, but we never seemed to spend too much time together. He's a big, strong quiet kid from Michigan. The Tigers paid him a bonus and

126

are pretty high on him. He's younger than I am, but he's very intelligent and is good company. I think we're going to hit it off very well together.

After looking over the apartment, which was unfurnished, we decided to take it. The price was $130 a month for the two bedroom apartment, utilities included.

Next, we headed for the minor leaguer's department store, the Salvation Army, to buy our furniture—a couple of mattresses, pillows, a sofa and some miscellaneous stuff. It came to $25.

We then went shopping to lay in a supply of groceries. In town, we ran into Rich Lawson, a pitcher who had played here last year. We asked him a million questions, especially concerning the weather.

"Cold?" Lawson said. "You guys cold? You must be kidding. Why it's at least thirty-eight degrees today, and in Clinton in April, that's a heat wave. Just wait 'til we go up north to Wisconsin Rapids next week. It's a hundred miles north of Milwaukee, right next to Green Bay. Last year we played one game in twenty-two-degree weather. Their catcher lost his toe because of frostbite."

In a desperate attempt to change the subject, I asked Lawson about the bus rides in the Midwest League.

"Bus rides, huh?" he said. "Lemme tell you guys 'bout bus rides in this league. We got six- to seven-hour bus rides to Rapids, Appleton, Decatur and Danville. We stay on the road all night long, get home at 6:00 A.M., and play the following night. It's great fun."

We left Lawson—not fast enough, I might add—and did our shopping and went to set up house. We were both getting hungry and all we had was canned food, so I went over to the landlord's apartment to borrow a can opener.

He and his wife inquired what kind of furniture we had and I said not very much. He immediately summoned his four or five kids and began barking orders and before I knew it, I was heading back to our apartment not only with a can opener, but with three chairs, a table, a tablecloth, assorted foods and groceries and meat, some pots and pans and a whole mess of things that were going to make our little apartment much more livable.

The hospitality was very unexpected, and greatly appreciated.

Clinton, Iowa
April 17

We had our first team meeting this afternoon and although I'm only in my second year of pro ball, I felt as though I had sat in on a dozen such meetings.

Len Okrie delivered a speech that was almost exactly the same as the one he gave us in Anderson last year, warning us about what we eat before a game, warning us to look out for the girls who were looking to latch on to a husband, telling us how he expected us to dress.

Len must have talked for twenty minutes and all during this time Carlos Quinones, a veteran infielder, was busy translating everything he said into Spanish for the half-dozen Latin American ballplayers. Every so often Ramon Vega, our pudgy, happy-go-lucky catcher, would break into a hearty laugh which needed no translation. Oke would stop talking and try to figure out what he had said that was so funny.

Finally, Carlos, trying to prevent an embarrassing scene, explained to Oke in his heavy accent, "Sheet, man, I no can translate everything you say, man." Oke just nodded.

After Okrie finished his talk, we were greeted by a businesslike little man who seemed to have a half-smoked cigar permanently wedged into the corner of his mouth. He also had a Clinton Pilot hat placed jauntily on his head and he was reading from a list as though reciting the menu of a restaurant.

His name was Fritz Colschen and he was the general manager of the club and his spiel pertained to the business rules of playing with the Pilots. He read aloud the ground rules, the cigar as natural an appendage of his face as his nose. He never once looked up from his sheet of paper. His voice just droned on in a monotone.

"No balls, no matter how scuffed or beat up, are to be given away to kids . . . EVER.

"Number 14—no broken bats are to be given away to kids . . . EVER.

"Number 15—all parts of your uniform are to be returned at the end of the season . . . nobody will receive a pay check until all parts of the uniform are accounted for . . . that includes your hats, especially. Nobody will keep his hat . . .

"Number 16. . . ."

At this point Tom Lantz, a pitcher who had played for Fritz before and who was listening to this diatribe while relieving himself, piped up from within the walls of the stall.

"Hey, Fritzie, you want me to return this piece of used toilet paper?"

Dubuque, Iowa
April 20

"OK, boys, this team up at Dubuque is a co-op team and they may be a little disorganized up there, so expect anything."

That was the only warning we got from Len Okrie. It was hardly sufficient.

Dubuque is an hour's ride through the cornfields of Iowa and, like Clinton, it is situated right on the banks of the Mississippi. Also like Clinton, the ballpark is right on the banks of the river, separated from the downtown area by the railroad tracks. That's where the similarity ends.

We got off the bus, already dressed in our road uniforms (which, I might add, mysteriously look more like Chicago Cub uniforms than Detroit Tiger uniforms, leading me to assume that Clinton was once a Cub affiliate). We had to dress at home because Dubuque doesn't have locker rooms yet . . . or showers.

THOMAS

Len Okrie, my manager, has dedicated his life
to baseball.

We walked into the ballpark and my heart sank. People always jokingly talk about "cow pastures" to play on, but here's where the term originated.

I was still getting over the initial shock when the Dubuque manager informed us we couldn't take batting practice or infield because the sod had just been installed that afternoon.

I couldn't believe it, but sure enough you could see the demarcations between the strips of sod. Then I noticed a few kids walking around the dirt part of the infield with bags slung over their backs. Closer inspection revealed they were picking up rocks and stones from the infield and that their sacks were almost full.

But the show was only beginning. A three-man color guard marched out to deep center field to salute the Stars and Stripes during the playing of the National Anthem. In true military fashion, the three men barked some signals, stiffened their bodies and as the first familiar strains of the anthem began to blare out, the color guard saluted a barren flagpole in center field. Totally unbeknownst to the three servicemen, but in full view of 3,000 hysterical spectators, the flag was hoisted over in left field, not center.

The three men were staunchly saluting the thin, lonely flag pole and the chuckles began to give way to audible snickers. Finally, about halfway through the anthem one of the men, hearing the laughter, turned slightly to his left and saw his mistake. In a quick but ungraceful move, he turned around to face the now risen flag in left. Like a Three Stooges comedy, the other two, never taking their salute from their forehead, followed suit in an equally awkward and unmilitaristic motion.

By the end of the anthem, the crowd was roaring with delight and eagerly downing their beer, yelling for more. Their wishes were soon fulfilled when the Mayor of Dubuque went to the pitcher's mound to throw out the first ball. After a long buildup of his reputation and a bit of political campaigning, the mayor wound up and released an anemic pitch that bounced about fifteen feet in front of home plate. The Dubuque catcher, caught off guard, promptly missed the ball and the crowd roared again as the pitch rolled back to the stands and stopped. I never did find out if it was scored a passed ball or a wild pitch.

The game began and, after my disappointment on opening day in Anderson, I was happy to be selected to start at second over Lloyd Sprockett and Carlos Quinones.

For a first game, it had everything. We had fifteen hits and not only lost, we were routed, 11–6. Their shortstop, Mel Barrow, who played last year at Gastonia, hit a grand slam to clinch the victory, but that happened after the fight.

Al Newsome, our Georgia country boy, got picked off first in the middle of the game with the score close. After a brief rundown, Al was tagged out. But Noose was so upset at being picked off, he took his frustrations out on the first baseman, wedging his spikes in his chest. Bang! Instant fight.

Both benches emptied out onto the field, everybody buddying up with the smallest opposing player, and the first fight of the season was underway. Now, really, who has a fight on opening day?

What I remember best, though, was a curious little thing I discovered at second base. I noticed it while smoothing the dirt around the bag in about the seventh inning. It was barely perceptible and it was stripped down to just a few weak strands for branches, but there was no mistaking it. There it was, a stripling, a baby tree.

I tried to dig it out with my spikes, but when I couldn't do it, I found myself developing a true respect and passion for that lonely little tree. I thought to myself, "How is this possible? How can a tree be alive and well in the middle of an infield?"

I was delighted with my find and, with my chest swelling with pride, I yelled over to shortstop, Tom Thompson.

"Hey, Tom, there's a tree growing over here at second base."

Tommy just looked at me as though I were crazy. But I can tell you if you ever go to Dubuque and if you get to second base, you'll find a tree growing there.

We played under the lights for the first time at Clinton, and two things of interest happened. We tied the Midwest League record by turning five double plays and we got streaked.

It happened in the seventh inning (the streaking, not the double plays) and it must have been all of about 30° when some kid did his thing, running from right to left field. I was wearing long underwear, about four sweatshirts, gloves and a jacket and I was still freezing, so this kid must have been one big goose pimple.

He scampered across the outfield, right past Al Newsome in left field, then up the foul pole and out of the ballpark. After the inning, Newsome came back into the dugout and exclaimed in his deep southern drawl, "Never seen anything like that before."

"What do you mean, Al, don't they have streakers in Georgia?"

"Sho' do, plenty of 'em, but this is the first time ah've seen one wearing a jacket."

Pay day today and there's good news. I guess somebody must have felt sorry for me, because my paycheck was larger than I thought it would be. It seems they've given me my $150 a month raise, after all. I'm up to $650 a month now. Hopefully, I can save some money this year, maybe clear $1,000 for the summer.

CLINTON

MID-WEST LEAGUE

CLASS "A"

AFFILIATE
DETROIT TIGERS

**1974
OFFICIAL
SCORE
BOOK**

№ 2042

PRICE
15¢

CLINTON PILOTS

PILOTS AT HOME

APRIL
21—2:30 p.m.—DUBUQUE
22-23—BURLINGTON
24-25—WISC. RAPIDS
30—WATERLOO

MAY
1—WATERLOO
2-3—APPLETON
8-9—DUBUQUE
14-15-16—DANVILLE
17-18—CEDAR RAPIDS
24-25—DECATUR
28-29-30—QUAD-CITIES
31—BURLINGTON

JUNE
1—BURLINGTON
2-3-4—WISC. RAPIDS
10-11—WATERLOO
12-13-14—APPLETON
20-21—DUBUQUE
27-28—DANVILLE
29-30—CEDAR RAPIDS

JULY
1—CEDAR RAPIDS
6-7—DECATUR
10-11—QUAD-CITIES

JULY
12-13-14—BURLINGTON
15-16—WISC. RAPIDS
24-25-26—WATERLOO
27-28—APPLETON

AUGUST
3-4-5—DUBUQUE
11-12—DANVILLE
13-14—CEDAR RAPIDS
20-21-22—DECATUR
26-27—QUAD-CITIES
29—DUBUQUE

July 22 - All Stars vs Iowa Oaks at Cedar Rapids, 7:30 p.m.
July 23 - Open Date

IT'S FUN TO BE A FAN

The Georgia Cracker, Al Newsome, walked into the clubhouse twirling a toothpick and wearing a wide grin and just dying for somebody to ask him why he was so happy.

I've always been a good straight man for him, so I asked.

"Hey, what's up, Noose—you're grinning like a Cheshire cat."

"Nothin' much, jus' found me a litt' ol' place to reside."

"Oh, really, where's that?"

"Right above Gabe and Walker's Bar and Lounge, right over yonder on Main Street."

"That sounds pretty good."

"You bet yo' sweet butt, boy. Everything I need is in easy walkin' distance . . . just downstairs."

You've seen in the morning paper, under the "Standings of the Clubs" and "Yesterday's Results," when a game is rained out, a line such as, "Clinton at Dubuque, ppd. rain."

Well, we got to Dubuque in plenty of time for the first game of our two-game series tonight and the weather was beautiful, but just as we arrived at the railroad crossing near the ballpark, a freight train was passing. So we waited . . . and waited . . . and waited . . . .

After about a half hour of viewing boxcars, we started to count them. We got to 200, then stopped. About forty-five minutes later, I began to wonder if we weren't tuned in on an instant replay of a jammed tape machine. Either that or the trains were running on a circular track and we were seeing the same cars over and over.

Then, to compound matters, the train got as weary as we

135

were and just stopped dead in its tracks. It sat there, exhausted, no doubt.

Ken Houston, our trainer, piped up and said, "Last year we had to wait two hours for a train to go by. The game had to be postponed because we got there late."

I thought of that happening to us and wondered, if it did, would they put under "Yesterday's Results" in the morning paper, "Clinton at Dubuque, ppd. train"?

Dubuque, Iowa
May 5

We finished our two-game series here and I just want to report that my little tree is still there and that a few small green leaves are beginning to appear on it.

I thought about writing a best-selling novel about my tree. How does this sound for a title—*A Tree Grows In Dubuque?*

Danville, Ill.
May 12

When we returned to the motel after the game, Tom Thompson, my roommate in spring training and one of my closest friends in baseball, told me that he was leaving to go to Lakeland. The shortstop down there had broken his leg and Thompson had been selected to be his replacement.

Tom was a valuable member of our team and we worked well together as a double-play combination. He had just gotten settled in Clinton, bought a new stereo set, met some nice girls, was furnishing his apartment and, most important, was doing well professionally. That night he had homered, doubled and singled.

Nevertheless, at 10:30 P.M., Tom packed his bags, shook hands with his teammates and left to return to Clinton. He

136

would get there around 4:00 A.M., pack his stuff and leave the same day for Florida, about 1,000 miles away.

As I wished Tom well, it gave me an empty feeling. I never knew him until spring training and now I was wondering if we'd ever see each other again. It made me realize how transient baseball friendships can be.

Decatur, Ill.
May 13

"Hey, Wolffie," shouted Ian Fink. "Don't forget to say hello to Abe Lincoln when you go outside. You know he comes from these parts."

I've always been one to go along with a gag, so I said sure.

We walked through the clubhouse, out through the stands and onto the field. We strolled up to the stands and behind the screen, sitting a few rows up, there he was. Abraham Lincoln. I couldn't believe my eyes. It was staggering. The guy looked just like Lincoln.

"Hey, Abe, what's happening, buddy?" said Ian, and for a minute, I said to myself, that's no way to talk to that man.

I was thunderstruck. The elderly, dignified man slowly and deliberately got up from his seat. His long, thin face was fringed by a bushy beard and his dark eyes were sincere and piercing. He was attired in a most respectable dark, three-piece suit. I looked for his stovepipe hat. Sure enough, there it was on the seat next to him and as he rose, he reached over and grabbed the hat and placed it on his head.

Talk about surrealism. Here I was on a Sunday afternoon in Decatur, Illinois, decked out in my baseball monkey suit and I'm looking at Abraham Lincoln. I thought he was going to begin saying, "Four score and twenty years ago . . . ."

Hey, I'm not fooling. The old man looked so much like the real thing, I had goose bumps. Ian explained to me that Abe attended all the games and was a retired railroad engineer.

137

But this guy really had me. I found myself with my cap in my hand, watching my language and addressing him as "Sir."

"My son," he said, "I have come to be a great judge of character during my years on this earth and I have arrived at the conclusion, even after this short conversation, that you are, and will become, something special."

I thanked him profusely, but asked him how he could predict such a thing.

"I can tell by some simple, but terribly profound indicators. For example, the way you talk to me, the way you handle yourself, the way your eyes look straight at me and even by the dimple in your chin. All I can inform you is that you're bound, in your lifetime, to be successful and achieve great accomplishments."

I beamed, thanked him again, and sprinted with Ian to the outfield to join the others in calisthenics.

Maybe instead of struggling to hit .250 in a Class A league, I should have asked Abe for a cabinet post or an ambassadorship.

Clinton, Iowa
May 18

Linda paid a visit, the first visitor I've had at Clinton. We had a five-game home stand and it just happened to coincide with Linda's vacation from Dartmouth Medical School, so I suggested she might like to come up and spend a few days and she did.

Before going to med school, Linda had majored in art history at Radcliffe, which is where I met her. After her disastrous visit to Anderson last year, I was hoping I could make a better showing this time and let her fully understand just what attracted me to baseball.

She's been here four days and in that time I've played fairly well, much better than I did during her visit to Ander-

138

son. Linda made a concerted effort this year to show me how much she understood baseball by attempting to keep score at each game.

I guess it's a prerequisite to understand the rules of the game and what actually happens if you want to keep score. So, when Linda attempted to keep track of all that happened on the field, she decided to devise her own little system of keeping score and she was very proud of her ingenuity.

One day I picked up one of her scorecards and tried to decipher her little symbols as to what had happened in the previous game. I'm an old scorekeeper myself, and it turned out that I not only couldn't decipher what happened, but the score page looked like a piece of work by Pablo Picasso.

It was just a complete mess of what looked like medical terms combined with art symbols and I had no idea what had happened in the game. I couldn't even figure out who had played or what position they played.

It turned out that if she didn't know somebody's name, she would just put down adjectives to describe what the guy looked like, which I thought was rather original. She also used swirls and little curls for base hits, things of that nature. She also told me that if she thought the umpire had called a play the wrong way, she just wrote it her way.

How I wish it were that easy.

Waterloo, Iowa
May 20

Forgive me for saying it, but now I know how Napoleon felt. I just met my Waterloo.

Because of poor weather, we hadn't played in four days. And because Oke has been alternating me with Lloyd Sprockett, I hadn't played in eight days when I got the call today. It had rained all day and there was no batting practice and so I went to the plate cold.

OFFICIAL BATTING ORDER

CLUB _____ DATE _____ 19__

No.	Name	Pos.	R.	LS.	V.
1.	JACKSON	6			
2.	Gregory	8			
3.	NEWSOME	7			
4.	Vega	2			
5.	VAZQUEZ	9			
6.	NATCHEZ	3			
7.	WOLFF	4			
8.	HANSEN	5			
9.	MOORE	1			
10.		P			
11.					
12.					
13.					
14.					
15.					
16.					
17.					
18.					
19.					
20.		P			
21.					
22.					
23.					
24.					
25.					

MANAGER

THOMAS I

Am I in there tonight?

In my first at-bat, I struck out, although I got three pretty good rips. My second at-bat I was ready. I got my eye back and worked the count to 3–2. I got right on top of the plate to guard it and the pitch came in low and away. I know it was low and away because I had to lean over quite a bit to see it.

"Streee-rike threeeee!" the umpire squealed.

Naturally, I had a few choice comments to make to him.

In my third at-bat, I was super-determined to hit the ball somewhere. Again I worked the count to 3–2 and crowded the plate. This time I watched the pitch come in high and tight. I held my ground, then pulled my head out of the way at the last split second.

"Steee-rike threeeee!" shouted the umpire, sounding like a broken record.

Now I had just gotten the hat trick, three K's in one game, and I let the ump have it, but good. After listening to my barrage, he threatened me.

"One more word out of you and you're gone," he warned.

I mused over this option, then replied: "The way I'm going tonight, that wouldn't be a bad idea."

The ump smiled and countered: "Just for that remark, you're in for the remainder of the game."

Now for my fourth at-bat. We were trailing, 1–0, in the eighth when I came to bat with runners on first and second. I worked the count to 3–1, then laced an outside fast ball down the right-field line. It curved foul by inches.

The count was 3–2 again. The fans were on me now and as I stepped back into the batter's box, I gazed at the ump. He was looking straight at me and I swear I saw a grin on his face.

Now I was set. This was going to be the pitch that would make or break my night. The pitcher wound up and threw his fast ball. I swung and here's how it was reported in the newspaper:

The Royals' big save was by second baseman Dan Hansen when he back-handed a line drive off the bat of Rick Wolff with two Pilots on base and two out in the eighth.

Joe Torre says that the hardest thing in baseball is "to learn that you're going to fail seven out of ten times." I think he's right, but knowing that doesn't take the sting out of failing. No matter how philosophical you get, it still hurts not to succeed.

Quite frankly, I haven't been playing well. I'm trying just as hard as before, but somehow things aren't dropping in.

The other day, Kevin Slattery and I were talking to some sixth-graders at an elementary school. They were amazed when we told them we got paid about $20 a game.

"Don't you ever play for fun?" a cute little girl asked.

Now, how do you answer a question like that?

Clinton, Iowa
May 29

I'm in a terrible hitting slump, the worst of my life. What's particularly frustrating about it is I know what I'm doing wrong at the plate, but I just can't seem to adjust to it.

Sometimes I see batters on our team, usually the younger players, who keep making the same mistake at bat. These kids have all hit .400 or so in high school against high school pitching, but when they get to pro ball they can't make the adjustment. They have never seen curve balls and sliders before, or learned how to hit the outside pitch. All they know is that they used to hit home runs in high school and now they can't understand why they can't even hit their weight.

Eventually, if they are any good, they learn to go with the pitch, poking the outside pitch to the opposite field. If they don't learn, they go home.

As far as I'm concerned, it's even more depressing. Being a bit older and having had the opportunity to learn from some good hitting instructors, I've learned how to follow the curve

142

ball and hit it to right; how to uppercut the low ball; how to wait on a pitch and slap it to the opposite field; how to think like a pitcher at bat; in short, I think I've learned a lot about the art of hitting.

Of course, execution and learning are two totally different concepts and even though I know how to adjust, I'm having difficulty doing so.

For example, tonight I grounded out three times and popped up to right. As a hitter, I realize a ground ball means I wasn't waiting on the pitch long enough—if I wait a split second longer on my swing, I should hit a line drive. So I adjusted and I popped up, which indicates I swung too late and that I dipped my back shoulder instead of swinging level.

The net result was an 0-for-4, a hitless night, simply because I couldn't adjust fast enough. Maybe if I had gotten a fifth time, I would have adjusted myself properly and gotten a hit, executing the way I should.

If a batter adjusts on each at-bat, hitting becomes terribly easy. Mike Hargrove proved that last year with Gastonia. It wasn't that he had superior physical ability, it was just that mentally he adjusted better than anyone else, and he made hitting look simple.

I know what I'm doing wrong. Len Okrie knows what I'm doing wrong because I had the same problem at Anderson last year and Len pointed it out to me then and now. All I have to do is think about what I want to do on each pitch and make my body do it, and I should be swinging right again.

There's no question that hitting is a precise science and a hard one to perfect. Hitting a baseball thrown at anywhere from 75 to 90 miles an hour from sixty feet, six inches away, is the hardest thing to do in sports. But there's no reason to make it harder than it already is. All I have to do is adjust, and I'll be out of this slump. It's not a question of desire. I've never tried harder in my life. I work at self-control, tell myself to relax and concentrate. I know I can do the job at bat and in the field; I proved that to myself last year against the same caliber of competition, and yet it's just not happening.

Tonight I hesitated on a play in the field. I came in for a slow bouncer with a runner moving from first to second. I guess I should have made the tag, but decided at the last moment to flip to second. My throw was a little off line and the runner was safe. We had a chance for two and got none.

At the plate on one of my at-bats, I lunged for a curve that broke a foot wide of the plate, then on the next pitch made myself look even worse by striking out on a ball that broke in the dirt. It's almost like self-torture.

I was horse-collared for the night and my average has now sunk to .190. Lloyd Sprockett, the other second baseman, has been alternating with me. And still another second baseman, a free agent with professional experience named John Rockwell, has begun working out with us and is expected to sign a contract. Not exactly the situation to restore one's self-confidence.

Three second basemen. I can feel the ax being sharpened. I hope I'm in there tomorrow. But will I get the chance? It's no fun being involved in your own soap opera.

Clinton, Iowa
May 30

Oke might have benched me and sent me packing in shame and humiliation and I couldn't have blamed him. But there I was in the starting lineup. It was as if he was giving me one last chance, and it gave me a big lift.

I hit the first pitch thrown to me so hard I could feel it to my spikes. All the frustration of the last few weeks went into my swing and the ball went soaring out to deep right center as I raced around the bases for a triple.

I added a solid single before the night was over and pulled off some nifties in the field, including a leaping grab of

tter play the batter a little to my right.

THOMAS DeFEO

a line drive to my right. We won the game and I know I made a solid contribution.

It's like getting a stay of execution, and I thank whoever it was who called the governor for me.

A full day of baseball. Five of us took extra batting practice starting at 10:00 A.M.

Oke had us each hit a basket of baseballs, one by one, off a stationary tee into the backstop screen. Oke put one ball after another on a hose-like rubber device built high off the ground and the idea was to focus on the ball and hit it as squarely and as hard as possible. The sun was steaming and the sweat just rolled down as we took swing after swing.

It was good practice, though. After a while I had my swing grooved to the point where I was making constant contact.

After a couple of hundred rips at this practicing device, Len moved out to the mound and we took more cuts against his pitching, finishing up around noon.

I was dripping wet and so were the others. I showered, went home, dozed for a couple of hours, got up, had a light snack, and went back to the ballpark for more.

Back in uniform by 5:00 P.M., more batting practice, infield drill and then the ball game. During the game I just couldn't shake the heaviness out of my arms and whip the bat like I wanted to. But I felt confident and in a good groove.

In the field, I started two double plays and both were important to Elliott Moore, who pitched our first shutout of the season. It was the first time the Quad-Cities team has been whitewashed this year and the first loss for their pitcher, Frank Panick, after six wins. I came out of the game feeling I had contributed to the victory.

146

Yesterday afternoon I spent some time talking with Len Okrie. He knows of my concern with my play and that of the team. Len feels that the ball club is just not playing up to its potential and that we've got to pull ourselves together and do the job.

After talking with him I ran into Ray Gimenez, our stocky, power-hitting right fielder. We discussed the team's play and came to the mutual decision that it might he helpful if we called a team meeting, with just the players attending. So we asked Len if we could have a ten-minute talk with the players before the game.

Len gave our idea his full approval and when we got to the ballpark, Oke gave a short pep talk, then gave the floor to Ray and me. Then he left.

Ray talked first. I tried to gather my thoughts and come up with something profound to try to impress the guys with some invigorating ideas.

Ray is a Puerto Rican who grew up in New York. That's not the usual background for a speech major, but Ray delivered the most sincere, most appealing speech I've ever heard in a clubhouse. It was down to earth, meaty and hard-hitting.

By the time he had finished, I felt anything I could have added would have been anticlimactic. I sputtered out a few lines, then opened the floor for discussion. Nothing else was said. Ray had said it all.

Despite our clubhouse meeting, we're still having trouble winning. After our five-game winning streak of a week ago, we've now lost five in a row and we're fading in the first-half race. Talk about the roller coaster existence of baseball.

Worse than that, I haven't been playing much lately. It's

147

tough enough to look at the line-up card and find you didn't make it, but then you sit on the bench and wonder how permanent this situation is going to be.

There's been a change in the second-base situation. Lloyd Sprockett has been sent to Lakeland and John Rockwell, who's been working out with us, has been signed and he started at second base tonight.

I got a chance to pinch-hit in the top of the ninth with two out. I decided to get my three rips, but after a few pitches and fouling off some, I walked on a 3–2 count. The next batter, Billy Michael, hit a long double and I scored from first. We lost the game, but at least I had the consolation of doing something productive.

I saw in today's paper that the Tigers had made their first draft pick, an infielder from California. If he signs, he will probably go either to Bristol or Clinton. If he comes to Clinton, they will have to make room on the roster for him, so my career is in serious jeopardy.

The field here is blessed with short fences and the ball carries extremely well. During batting practice, a few balls were hit out and then the razzing began, with me in the middle of it.

"C'mon Wolffie, let's see you pound one out," chided my roomie, Jeff Natchez.

"Hey, Wolff, downtown, man, go downtown," egged on Carlos Quinones in his pigeon English.

Even Okrie, who was throwing BP, got in on the act. "Where do you want it, son? Just tell me where."

Naturally, when I try to hit a home run, all I produce is a pop-up. My swing is geared to hitting down on the ball, hitting line drives and grounders, not fly ball home runs. And after I hit a few pop-ups, the guys all laughed at my futility as I left the cage.

But during the game, the impossible happened in the seventh inning. I don't know what I did differently; all I recall was swinging at a fast ball and the next thing I saw was a high fly heading for downtown Wisconsin Rapids. A home run! I instantly went into my home-run trot, which you may recall, I have not had an opportunity to perfect, and when I reached home, I burst into a huge grin.

To my amazement—not to mention my chagrin and disappointment—nobody was there to congratulate me. Everybody was sitting in the dugout, seemingly preoccupied with other things. Then it occurred to me that I was getting the silent treatment.

So I strolled over to the dugout, casually put my helmet back on the rack, and quietly took my seat on the bench.

Suddenly, the guys erupted in laughter, grabbing me and shaking me so hard I thought I'd be pulled apart. That was such great fun, I promised myself I'd try to do it again.

The thrill of the home run was short-lived, however. Rapids' shortstop, Ron Farkas, hit a two-run homer in the last inning to tie the game and two innings later Farkas drove in the winning run with a single, dropping us to our seventh straight defeat.

Clinton, Iowa
June 11

Oke has given me permission to fly to Cambridge for my graduation at Harvard University. There's a full week of pomp and ceremony, but the actual commencement exercises are Friday morning, June 13. I assured Oke I'd be back in uniform in time to play against Appleton that night and, with that stipulation, he gave his OK.

I'm back and the events of the last twenty-four hours are almost mind-boggling when you realize that at noon today I was rubbing elbows (in cap and gown) with Ralph Ellison, Beverly Sills and Derek Bok, and that eight hours later, I was rubbing elbows (in my Pilots' baseball uniform) with Al Newsome, Elliott Moore, Jeff Natchez and Greg Kuhl.

The whole thing was very James Bondian.

I arrived in Boston early this morning and attended my graduation, everything going off fine. The return trip was a little more hairy.

I boarded a plane in Boston at 3:00 P.M. and the flight was fine. I slept over an hour, conking out from exhaustion after all the excitement of the graduation at Harvard. Everything was going smoothly, I was right on schedule to make the start of the game, until the captain's voice came over the PA system.

"Ladies and gentlemen, there seems to be a traffic jam over O'Hare Field in Chicago. We have been placed in a hold position for landing."

Instant panic! I have to be in Clinton at 7:00 P.M. for a 7:30 game. I can't afford to be stuck over Chicago.

About a half hour later, with me in a nervous sweat and chomping on my nails feverishly, we finally landed. It was 4:50, Chicago time. I raced through the terminal, got my suitcase and my rented car and I was off. All of this consumed about twenty minutes, putting me on the road to Clinton at 5:15.

It's a two-and-a-half-hour drive from Chicago through the cornfields to Clinton at legal speed, but I must have set new land speed record racing there, dodging trucks and passing slow pokes moving at a mere 50 miles an hour.

I was fighting against time and I knew I was in a hopeless cause. I was going as fast as I dared, but now I was praying for rain, hoping the game would be postponed, or at least delayed. But the skies were clear, my prayers were hopeless.

I continued to drive, plotting my next move. At 6:45, I was still about seventy miles from Clinton, so I decided to stop and call Fritz Colschen, the GM. I wasted about three minutes with the operator and finally got a busy signal. The operator explained that the telephone I was calling had been left off the hook.

Now I was really in a panic. In fact, my panic was rapidly giving way to suffocating paranoia. I was going to be late, no doubt of it. Okrie would be furious and I can't get through to the ballpark because the phone is off the hook.

I decided to call radio station KROS, hoping to contact the Pilot broadcaster, Hank Dihlmann, and ask him to tell Okrie I would be late. I couldn't get Hank because he was starting his pre-game show.

I hopped back in the car and just rationalized as best I could, trying to convince myself that the new second baseman, Rockwell, would have to play his third straight game at second base.

When I got within forty miles of Clinton, I heard a familiar voice on the radio. I had the pre-game show on and the voice belonged to Fred Swanson. He had just been activated from the Bristol roster and I couldn't understand the change. Something must be up.

Then Hank gave the starting lineup and I almost drove my car off the road when I heard it.

"Leading off for the Pilots, Steve Litras, second base . . ."

Litras? He's got a bad arm, he can't play. Where's Rockwell?

Hank continued. ". . . Steve is playing second base tonight despite a bad arm because John Rockwell decided to quit pro ball yesterday and Rick Wolff has yet to return from his graduation ceremonies at Harvard."

I was helpless. I was twenty-five miles away, yet I couldn't do a thing. Then, just as the National Anthem was being played, I thought how Okrie must have been cursing me because I promised I'd be there by game time.

Then I got a merciful break. Just before the game was about to start, it began to rain. Hank reported that the game was going to be delayed and with this break from the gods, I sped onward through Morrison and Fulton, Illinois.

I went racing through the rain, getting closer all the time, and when I saw the landmark of Clinton, the gigantic cement Mr. Peanuts silo, sticking up in the middle of the green trees of Clinton like a huge monolith, I knew my battle was nearly won.

I crossed the Mississippi River, spying the lights of the ballpark, then raced through town, pulled into the parking lot, hopped out of the car and raced into the ballpark. The locker room door was locked, so with the bravado of a movie star, I raced into the stands and down into the box seats, right above the Clinton dugout.

The game was just starting. It had been delayed a half hour by the rain. I ran to the wall and jumped over the dugout and plopped right in front of Len Okrie, who was calmly chewing on a toothpick.

I couldn't even talk I was so out of breath. I still had my Harvard tie on and my suit clothes and Oke simply asked if I had a good time. I blurted out an apology and ran in and got dressed for work.

In the sixth inning I was called on to pinch-hit. How nice it would be to get a hit and celebrate my graduation. I struck out.

What more can I say? I had come halfway across the country, from Boston to Chicago to Clinton, racing at top speed, just to get to the ballpark in time to strike out.

152

At four o'clock, just a few hours before our game with Appleton, clouds from the Land of Oz began to whirl around and blot out the sky. The radio and TV were scratched out by static from lightning and thunder and so, fearing the worst, for it was beginning to look like tornado weather, Jeff, his mother, who was here for a visit, and I began to look for shelter.

By the time Mrs. Natchez had descended the stairs from our apartment, the rain had already started, accompanied by hailstones. The sky was black as night and the wind literally whipped at up to 60 miles an hour. I yelled at Jeff from our porch to hurry. It was getting serious outside.

"I can't leave quite yet," said Jeff from the bathroom. "Nature's calling."

"I tell you, Jeff, nature's calling outside as well."

I fled, imploring Jeff to hurry and be sure to slam the door. By the time I arrived at a place for safety, I could see Jeff running down the stairs in a mass of ice balls. As soon as he reached us, I saw our front door fly open. There was nothing we could do about it now.

Half an hour later, the storm blew over. I went outside and found enough hail to make ice cubes. We checked our front door. The kitchen and living room were under a foot of water. With the game called off, we would be kept busy during the night mopping up.

Since we last played Dubuque, the Packers have acquired my old roomie, George Cappuzzello, and Mike Corbett, an outfielder who played briefly in Anderson last year. It was like a class reunion with Cappy and Corby being the center of attention.

You can tell a minor league park by the signs
on its fences, and the Illinois Central in Dubuque
is a bonus.

As I talked with Cappy, I couldn't help feeling he would have preferred to be wearing the road gray of Clinton instead of the home white of Dubuque.

The game was exciting, particularly for two last-place teams. It was very cold, more like April than June, and the lead kept changing hands. Corbett got revenge on his teammates with a homer that tied the score, 3–3, and we eventually went ahead on Ramon Vega's two-run double. But starter Tom Lantz tired in the ninth and the Packers tied the score, 5–5.

It remained that way until the eleventh, when I led off with a triple to right, then scored on Bill Michael's single, and Greg Kuhl came in to preserve the victory.

At one point, we had Steve Vasquez at third, Carlos Quinones at short, Luis Atilano at first and Ramon Vega catching. I felt like Henry Kissinger on a trip to Latin America.

Let me get back to Greg Kuhl, our relief pitcher, for a moment. You may remember that this spring his name appeared on Hoot Evers' "cut" list and, if you do, you may be wondering how come he's still here. That's a story in itself.

In essence, Greg has returned from the dead. His name had been called out over the PA in Tigertown, although he had pitched well in two years in the minors. He went to Hoot's office and Hoot was telling him, "I'm sorry, but we have to let you go" and so on and so forth.

Greg is only twenty and he was emotionally broken up at the news. He wanted so much to make it, had put a lot into the game and really wasn't doing that badly. He asked Hoot if he could come back in ten or fifteen minutes, after he had gotten hold of himself, and talk things over. Hoot said OK.

So, Greg went out and while he was gone, Evers apparently went back to the file and looked up Greg's record. Greg walked around, calming himself and preparing himself for his release. But when he returned to Evers' office, a strange thing happened.

"Greg, I tell you," Hoot said. "I've looked over your

155

The visitors' clubhouse at Dubuque is a far cry
from Tiger Stadium.

records again and decided that I'll give you one more chance this year to show what you can do. You've done a good job for me in the past and I think I'll give you one more year."

Greg couldn't believe his ears. He thanked Hoot and promised him he wouldn't regret it and Greg is pitching like he aims to keep his promise.

Okrie put Greg in the bullpen and he's become one of the top relief pitchers in the league. He has an excellent record, his earned-run average is under two and he's the workhorse of our staff. He's a good relief pitcher. He has the right temperament for that job, he possesses a good slider and he's at his best in tough situations.

Dubuque, Iowa
June 16

Here we are in the middle of June and the temperature is about 48 degrees.

We won again, 3–1, as Larry Feola pitched a fine game and got some excellent defensive help from the infield as we turned three double plays, all coming at propitious times.

It was really cold out there. I had to pull out my long underwear again, sweatshirts and batting gloves. The fellows from Puerto Rico were really going crazy, for they never play ball in such cold weather. But the starting infield of experienced ballplayers—Atilano, Wolff, Quinones and Vasquez—was able to cope with the conditions and perform well.

I was 1–for–3 with a walk and a run scored. As long as I keep scoring runs and making the plays in the field, my batting average becomes less important. I flied to right, struck out on a good, hard slider and blooped a hit over the first baseman's head.

It was a classic example of bat control, a la Manny Mota. The guy had me 0–2 as I fouled off the first two pitches. Then he threw me another excellent slider on the black. I swung, but seeing the ball break away, I had nothing to do but lit-

157

erally throw the bat at the ball and, presto, a base hit to right. Nothing to it.

The real star of the game was my roomie, Jeff Natchez, who suddenly is coming into his own. Jeff is six foot three and he weighs 195. He's got the size and all the other tools to be a major leaguer, plus the fact he's from Michigan. The Tigers are very high on him and they are waiting for him to fulfill his enormous potential.

Jeff is a physical fitness nut. During the off season he keeps in shape by lifting weights and running a lot. Since I've been rooming with him, I've learned how nutty he can be about fitness. He'll get up early in the morning after playing a night game the night before and go out and play tennis for a couple of hours, then he'll go to the Y and work out and run and be ready to play baseball at night.

When we go on road trips, he not only takes his clothes, he actually packs his weights and he'll lift them in the hotel room during the day.

At first Jeff seems to be kind of tight, introverted. He doesn't have much to say. But when you get to know him, he's easy to talk to and he's not shy about speaking right up.

Of course, nobody really gives him much lip. If they did, they'd be taking their life in their hands.

Last year, Jeff was only twenty years old at Anderson and he had a tendency to take too many pitches and too long a stroke. As a result, he struck out quite a bit. Yet he had quite a few RBIs, did an excellent job in center field and showed some power at times.

This year, he has improved tremendously. He's cut down on his stroke and he jumps on the first good pitch more often. He's raised his batting average about 40 points by learning to go with the pitch and hit the outside pitch to right. And he's helped himself become a more well-rounded player by doing a good job at first base when he's needed there. You can see that

158

oommate at Clinton was outfielder
atchez.

LARRY MAY
(CLINTON HERALD)

a year of maturity and experience have made quite a difference in him.

Natch got four hits tonight, raising his average to a staggering .260 or so. Jeff confessed that having so high an average in June was a new experience for him.

He hit four shots for base hits, none of them cheapies, and it's possible that he made more progress in one night than he has in two years.

What was the difference? Nothing really complex. Jeff was simply being aggressive at the plate, attacking the first good pitch he saw instead of waiting and then having to hit the pitcher's pitch.

Jeff has always been a kind of baseball enigma because of his build, which can best be described as being like that of a Trojan warrior. His metabolism is unbelievable. He's the only guy I know who can work up an appetite while eating.

Quad-Cities
June 18

Georgia's gift to the Midwest League, Al Newsome, is on a hot streak. He hit safely again tonight, giving him a streak of hitting safely eighteen of his last nineteen games. He's closing in on the league leaders in batting.

Quad-Cities
June 19

The honorary award, invented by our puckish trainer, Ken Houston, is called the "Nod of the Night." It consists of an old beat-up ball wrapped in white tape with "Nod of the Night" printed on it.

Its purpose is to honor the most outstanding event perpetrated by a Clinton player during that particular night's game . . . but only if we win.

This night, as we battled back to defeat the Quad-Cities Angels, 10–7, in ten innings, there were two nominees for the award, Al Newsome and me.

Here are our credentials: I had a particularly good game, getting two key hits off Angel pitcher Frank Panick to help obtain and preserve the lead. I also made a super play in the field, going behind second base to backhand a grounder and then flipping it to Quinones at second for an important force-out.

But that's not why I was nominated. I was nominated for my bat-throwing antics. No, I didn't throw my bat in disgust, I just threw it accidentally when I swung at a pitch in the game. The bat simply slipped loose from my grasp and spun away like a helicopter's propeller toward the third baseman.

What made it particularly humorous was that I did it not once, but three times. It got to be a joke. Panick would wind up, make the pitch and I'd swing and . . . whoosh! . . . the bat was headed for greener pastures. Okrie would have to retrieve the bat for me and the whole procedure would repeat itself.

Newsome was a candidate for a singular achievement. Although he was 0–for–5 at bat and helped transform some Angel singles into triples in the outfield, he was cited for a wonderful imitation of a fullback charging into a linebacker on a goal line stand.

The Angel catcher, Pat Kelly, is about six foot three, 220 pounds. Throughout the game, he had kept complaining to the umps about little insignificant things, called pitches, the lines of the batter's box, the bat throwing. This got to be a sore point with the Pilots and it wasn't long before our bench began to razz him badly.

He countered this by complaining to the umpire about our choice of obscene verbiage. This merely added more fuel to the flames and we were really hot on his tail.

Eventually, we got our big chance. Al, who was leading

the barrage on poor Kelly, got on base in the top of the tenth. With one out, Ray Gimenez singled, sending Newsome to third.

The Angels' infield was drawn in tight for a play at the plate as Luis Atilano hit a high hopper to second. The Angel second baseman fielded the sharply hit ball and fired it back home in an effort to head off the lead run as here came big ol' Newsome, rambling down the third-base line like a bee-stung bear.

Unfortunately for Kelly, the throw came in high and he had to leap for it. Newsome just set his sights and as Kelly caught the ball in mid-air, Newsome rammed into him like a fullback plunging for a TD, the moment of impact coming simultaneously for the ball and Newsome. It was a thunderous collision, these two big men colliding, but Newsome's advantage was that he was in motion. Kelly, who was standing firm and concentrating on getting the ball, was thrown back ten feet, losing the ball and his composure somewhat.

Big Al just brushed himself off and calmly walked over to our bench, where everyone was going wild with delight.

For this one act, Newsome won the "Nod of the Night," and I couldn't argue with the decision. Maybe if I throw a few more bats tomorrow night I'll get renominated.

Clinton, Iowa
June 21

If you pick up the Des Moines *Register,* you'll read "Dubuque at Clinton—Rain."

That's innocent enough, but as a description of what happened, it's about like saying there was a drizzle in Johnstown.

We were scheduled for a doubleheader against the Packers, starting at 6:30. The day had been brutally warm, the temperature hovering around 96 degrees with the humidity oppressive. It was the hottest, muggiest day of the year. It was so hot, in fact, that a summer thunderstorm seemed imminent.

162

Sure enough, by the time Jeff and I left our apartment at four o'clock, clad only in shorts and T-shirts, it was beginning to get dark off in the distance. And we could hear claps of thunder from far away.

It was still unbearably hot when we took the field for batting practice at five, the kind of evening when all you had to do was pick up one ground ball or swing a bat and you were drenched in sweat. It kept getting darker in the north as we labored through batting practice.

The Dubuque club arrived a few minutes later. Some of the Packers had dressed in their away uniforms. Others, anticipating a rainout, were still in street clothes.

Near the end of our batting practice, it began to rain, big globs of water splish-splashing on the field, drenching everything but not really cooling things off.

We finished BP in this rain shower and, picking up the balls and bats, scrambled off the field. It seemed certain the rain would continue for quite a while, but to our amazement, the rain suddenly stopped. I remember looking up at the sky and noticing that toward the north, up the river, the sky was pure black and ablaze with lightning.

It was scary. I ran down through the dugout, through the runway, up to the clubhouse and out through the stands. Running up to the top of the stands, I could feel the wind pick up, a wind that was getting stronger and fiercer each moment.

When the trees began to lose some leaves and my hat flew off, I decided it was time to take shelter. On the way back to the clubhouse, I heard Eddie Morrison, a pitcher from Missouri and a veteran of tornadoes, yelling at everybody to take cover.

"Everybody downstairs," he shouted, "down in the dugout or runway. This could be a twister."

On the way to the runway, which is under the reinforced concrete stands, I stopped to look at the ominous sky. The rain was now a driving force, unlike any rain I had ever seen before. It was actually raining too hard to see more than a few

163

hundred feet away. Yet the wind was blowing so hard, every-thing was bent at a horizontal angle parallel to the ground. The sky was black as midnight, although it was only 6:00 P.M., and the constant winds were so strong that the black clouds were skimming, it seemed, only a few feet off the earth.

I finally got too soaked and too scared and I ran for shelter. Everybody on the team was down below and a few spectators and a whole bunch of little kids had all huddled in the runway, which was beginning to fill with rainwater. I man-aged to get down to the dugout opening where Ed Morrison was standing and trying to calm everybody, especially the younger kids who were on the verge of tears. Eddie was calmly smoking a cigarette—at least he appeared calm to me.

I looked out on the field and saw our batting cage, which is on wheels, not just rolling but being driven like a truck by the wind toward the outfield fence. It abruptly smashed head-on into the iron fence with a large crash.

The wind was frightening. I was in awe of such raw nat-ural power. It was hard to comprehend. The light towers were shaking like so many grass reeds in the gale. The rain kept coming harder and harder and the wind, with its low black clouds, kept blowing stronger and stronger.

Just then the clubhouse door opened and down the run-way came Ian Fink, Bill Jackson and our two batboys. All four were drenched. They were frantic and Ian blurted out that down the road, about fifty yards away, somebody had been driving in his car when a wooden plank, about twelve feet long, had been ripped away by the wind from the bleachers of a nearby recreation field and been thrown through the wind-shield of his car, causing the driver to veer off the road and smash into a brick wall.

The guys saw that the driver was unconscious and bleed-ing profusely. The wooden plank had gone through the wind-shield and smashed out the back window. The car was totalled and unless the poor victim got help quickly, he was in danger of losing his life.

An ambulance was summoned, but it was virtually impossible to get around in the storm. All sorts of debris had filled the air, flying around and hitting everything. Trees had begun to fall outside the ballpark and the power was beginning to go out as the lights flickered.

We just waited in the semi-darkness of the runway, our feet beginning to get damp from the rain that was draining in. Everybody was concerned about the man in the car, but at that particular point in the storm, we were all completely helpless.

In about a half hour, the worst was over. The ambulance had arrived about ten minutes earlier for the man in the car, and the spectators in the runway with the team were beginning to trickle out of the clubhouse. We were all shaken, but we managed to strip down, shower and change.

Jeff and I dressed and went out into a steady drizzle. The sky was clearer now and the temperature had dropped about 25 degrees. We walked to the parking lot, which was strewn with leaves, tree branches and trees that had been blown over, and the whole asphalt lot now looked like a plush, green garden. Jeff's car was covered with all sorts of foliage and after scraping the leaves off, we got in and took off for home.

The town was one big disaster area. Trees by the hundreds were literally uprooted and thrown on the ground and against homes. Windows were smashed all over the place. Debris and garbage were scattered everywhere. Power lines were down all over the roads. All the power was out, no lights were on anywhere. People were emerging from their shelters, evaluating the damage to their homes and property.

Nobody, it seemed, had been untouched by the storm. Cars were ruined by heavy tree trunks that had fallen on them, floods were everywhere, and sewers were backing up. It was a nightmarish scene as Jeff and I rode back to our apartment.

We live on the second floor of a brick apartment house and the first thing we noticed was a broken window. The wind had been so strong that it ripped off a rubberized shingle from the roof and smashed it into our window. Glass was shattered over twenty feet in our kitchen, hall and bedroom. Picking up the guilty shingle, I couldn't believe it had done so much damage. It appeared to Jeff and me that a hard-thrown baseball wouldn't have caused so much destruction. Yet the window was a total loss and glass was all over the place, all due to a small shingle and the wind.

Our roof was leaking and the power was off. With the electricity gone, all our food was spoiled in the refrigerator. We had to buy candles for the night and the air conditioning was out. Eventually, we got it all cleaned up and straightened out.

Later, we heard that the man in the car had died in emergency surgery at the hospital. A man had lost his life only a few hundred yards away from us, all because of the storm.

Ray Gimenez, recently married, had his trailer demolished by the tornado. Len Okrie lost his trailer also. Nobody had any power and everybody had broken windows and leaky roofs. It was obvious it would take some time for things to get back to normal in Clinton.

And all it said in the paper was "Dubuque at Clinton—rain."

Decatur, Ill.
June 24

What a difference a day makes.

Yesterday, Clinton ended up in last place in our division as the first half of the split Midwest League season came to an end. Now, twenty-four hours later, we're in first place in our division, having won the first game of the second half of the race.

I also went from bottom to top when Len Okrie told me before the game that he was moving me from eighth in the batting order to leadoff. In my new spot, I went 2-for-5, scored a run and made some good plays in the field.

166

Batting first is more enjoyable because I can do a lot of things one doesn't do with the pitcher batting next. For example, I can be more selective on pitches since getting on base is the prime requisite for a leadoff man. When you bat eighth, you don't look for a walk because that leaves it up to the pitcher. There's also a good opportunity to steal bases. Batting eighth, one hesitates to do so for an out might have the pitcher leading off the next inning. And, of course, there's more opportunity to score runs leading off and, after all, that's what it's all about.

Psychologically, you can get your team off on the right foot by leading off with a base hit, as I did tonight in our 8–0 win. The victory put us in first place.

It's a nice feeling to look at the league standings and find you're leading the league.

Decatur, Ill.
June 25

We took over sole possession of first place in the Southern Division by beating Decatur for the second straight night. Everybody else has either lost or split their first two games.

We won, 4–3, in twelve innings and I had one of my best games. I got three hits and drove in the winning run in the top of the twelfth. I also made several good plays in the field, stole a base and scored a run.

My first at-bat, I bunted and was thrown out by a half-step. Next time up I was hit by the pitch. Third time around I hit a sharp grounder through the hole for a hit. My fourth at-bat, I was ordered to bunt a runner over. The fielders were charging in, expecting the bunt, so I quickly straightened up and blasted a line drive to left. It must have scared the daylights out of the Decatur third baseman, who was almost looking down my throat.

167

My last at-bat I came up with the winning run on second. I drilled another line shot to left to score the runner for the winning RBI.

It was a truly great game for Clinton and a memorable game for me. Why should this game be so difficult some days and so easy on others?

Clinton, Iowa
June 27

I'm feeling pretty good tonight. We beat Danville, 2–0, with Bill Jackson, an amiable guy from North Dakota, pitching an excellent game and getting good, tight defense.

I was 2–for–4, two singles, and made a few more excellent defensive plays. One, in particular, especially pleased me. It came late in the game, with one on and one out, when the leadoff batter for Danville, Dick Davis, hit a line shot, one-hopper right at me. I could do nothing but let the ball hit me squarely in the chest, try to recover and flip to second for the force-out. Quite a gutsy play if I must say so.

On the next pitch, the Danville batter hit another line drive to my right. I dashed over and grabbed it with one hand to end the inning. Sometimes I get as much kick out of making a good play in the field as I do out of hitting the ball on the nose.

I was feeling pretty good after the game. Our record was now 3–1 in the second half and I had slowly pulled my average up to about .235 after spending most of the season under .200.

But the thing that made me feel best was something that happened in the clubhouse after the game, something that is most unusual and has never happened to me before in pro ball.

The clubhouse is small and everybody is shouting and happy because we won. One of the directors of the team even

168

bought us a case of beer. A few reporters were walking around, most of them centering on Bill Jackson, who had just thrown the shutout.

I was stripping down to get in the shower when Bill Michael, our mischievous and adventurous center fielder, grabbed one of the reporters, took him over to me and loudly proclaimed, with all sincerity, "Here's the reason Clinton is doing so well. Rick here is doing it all for us, hitting, getting on base, scoring runs and cementing our infield together. I tell you Rick could be the next second baseman in Detroit."

I was stunned and embarrassed. I really didn't know what to say, so I thanked Bill and mumbled something about how the whole team was doing the job, not one man.

That's the beauty of pro ball. Sure it's nice to see your name in the headlines, but when your teammates publicly acknowledge to others and to you that they think you're doing a fine job, well, to me that's worth all the press clippings you've ever had. Peer recognition is the real thrill of baseball to me, the camaraderie and the achieving of a goal through a team effort. That's what baseball is all about.

Clinton, Iowa
June 28

Today is the Growler's birthday. He's seventy-nine. And commemorating the event, the front office and a couple of the players got together and decided to give him a birthday cake.

The Growler may be the most distinctive, most indispensable person associated with the Clinton Pilots. He certainly has seniority.

His real name is Earl Fenn, but you have only to listen to him to know why he is called the Growler. He is a small man, but his raspy voice booms out across any locker room or baseball field.

Growler can be found at the morning workouts usually

clad in a pair of old baggy work pants, a white shirt with the sleeves rolled up and an old Detroit Tiger cap from the Ty Cobb era perched on top of his bald head.

Growler will be sitting on one of the benches in the clubhouse with his legs crossed, smoking a cigarette, and he'll greet us as we troop in from the workout, drenched in perspiration from a couple of hours of strenuous work in the morning sun. As we cool off, Growler will begin to reminisce, beguiling us with stories about the days "when baseball players really cared about the game and were real ballplayers and gave all they had to win."

A usual conversation with Growler will start off about the 1960s, with Growler talking about ballplayers who have long since gone to the big leagues and retired. Eventually, he will make his way back to the 50s, back into the days of the old Three-I League, and then back into the 40s. He'll end up in 1910 when he was a ballplayer and he'll talk about the days when he used to slide into third base and third base was a boulder or something.

Growler says he has been at every ball game the Pilots have played at home for the last sixty years and there's certainly nobody around to dispute him. He sits with his cronies in what has become known as the "medicare section" of the ballpark, down the first-base line.

The purpose of the birthday cake was to honor him for his years of loyalty to the Clinton Pilots. The plan was to have him come out between the fifth and sixth innings at home plate for the presentation.

When the time came, Ken Houston went out with a gigantic cake, aided by Billy Michael, our center fielder. Ken gave a long and elaborate tribute to Mr. Growler Fenn for being a long-time loyal and dedicated fan of the Clinton Pilots.

The fans gave Growler a tremendous ovation and we waited for him to come down from the stands to receive his cake. After a couple of embarrassing moments, it became apparent that Growler was nowhere to be found.

170

THOMAS DeFEO

Growler) Fenn never misses a game.

After three or four minutes of embarrassed silence, here came Growler hustling on the field with a big smile on his face.

It was Growler's big moment and he almost missed it. When it came time for him to take center stage, Growler had been in the john.

The Des Moines *Register* orange sports page carries a roundup of Midwest League action with a small headline and a paragraph about each game.

In today's paper, the small type read: "Wolff's Single Rescues Clinton" and the one-sentence paragraph went on to describe how I drove in the winning run against Decatur.

I couldn't get too cocky about it, though. Topping the long column, just to the left of the game results, was a big, bold headline proclaiming: "Iowa Getting More Turkeys."

This "game" story got more space than the entire Midwest League.

Today was a beautiful day in Clinton. The sun was shining everywhere and there was a faint breeze in the air to keep things cool. I took advantage of this perfect day to get a little sun by sitting next to the banks of the glorious Mississippi. I could almost see Huck Finn and Tom Sawyer go by on their legendary raft. It was just a nice, serene setting.

My mind drifted back to last night's game, an 8–6 defeat by Cedar Rapids in ten innings. Just like O. Henry short stories, this Clinton team never seems to run out of surprise endings.

172

We battled back and forth, but after the Astros built up a 6–2 lead, the game looked like it was out of hand. Then I sliced a triple down the right-field line with a man on to make it 6–3 in the sixth and in the bottom of the eighth, with men on first and second, I even surprised myself by lining a double in the gap in left center.

All of a sudden, it was 6–5 and I'm the tying run on second. The partisan home crowd was really enthused and Carlos Quinones, the next batter and the hero of the previous night's game, stroked a single to center and I scored with the tying run.

The score remained tied at 6–6 until the tenth when the Astros got men on first and second with one out. The next batter sacrificed and with two out, they had men on second and third.

Greg Kuhl was pitching and seeing the Cedar Rapids' shortstop coming to bat, I ran to the mound and told Greg to try to pitch him high and tight because he was a slap hitter who tried to poke everything to right. Kuhl's first pitch was perfect, high and tight and surprising the batter, who leaped back in fright. The ball accidentally glanced off his bat with a peculiar spin down the first-base line.

The batter was still stunned after the close pitch, but he recovered and began running down the line. The runners, of course, were on the move, just in case the ball stayed fair. It appeared to be an easy out, a nice simple bouncer to Quinones at first. At worst, it was going to be a foul ball.

But Carlos, playing first in place of the injured Atilano, was caught helpless as the ball bounced over the bag, then glanced off his chest at a funny angle. He scrambled for the ball, but his toss to Greg, covering first, was too late, and two runs scored on what was a perfect pitch.

Another surprise ending for the Pilots. At least we're original.

173

After our good start in the second half, things are beginning to happen. Atilano hurt his elbow in a collision at first and may be lost for the season. Elliott Moore has been called up to Montgomery. Good for Elliott, bad for us.

We got three new players, all of them raw rookies. Ken Gregory is a young outfielder, Fred Austin a third baseman and Mel Jackson, the rawest of the three, is a shortstop and my new double-play partner.

Mel is a shy black from Chicago. He's an unassuming young man and in two games so far, he has shown that he has some of the basic ingredients to be a big leaguer. He can run and he can throw. Unfortunately, Mel has already made six errors in two games, most of them costly. He has a cannon for an arm, but he is going to have a problem until his nervousness wears off.

Tonight, for example, with the bases loaded and one out, Fred Mims (who played on the Pan-American team a few years back) hit a one-hopper to me. It was an easy double play ball and I gave Jackson a perfect feed. He responded by firing the ball in the general direction of first base. Quinones didn't have a chance as the ball sailed into the stands.

But, boy, what a throw. It was like a lightning bolt. If Mel can only control it, he'll be on his way.

We have just completed a very frustrating and bizarre three days, two here and one at home vs. Cedar Rapids.

First things first—in the Cedar Rapids game we were sailing along with a 2–0 lead in the fifth inning behind Tom

Lantz, who had his good, hard slider working right. All of a sudden, it became apparent that a heavy rainstorm was quickly heading our way.

All we had to do was get three more out and the game would be official, the victory ours even if it did rain. So we all urged Tom to work quickly and get the last three outs to assure the victory.

But luck was not on our side. The first Astro batter made out, but the second batter reached first with an infield hit. The next batter reached on an error.

By now the lightning and thunder were all over the place and between pitches our outfielders would kneel on one knee in order not to be lightning rods. You could actually see the rain in the distance, and it was getting closer.

All we needed was a quick double play to make it an official game, but Lantz walked the next batter to load the bases as the raindrops began to fall. The winds were swirling as the Cedar Rapids shortstop, a slap hitter, put one up in the air that seemed to soar like a balloon until it came down against the wall for a double and three RBIs. All of a sudden, the whole pitcure changed. Now we're the home team and the game isn't official until we have been to bat in the fifth and so we're saying, "Come on, rain, let's see it pour."

The rain did come and the game was washed out and the three Cedar Rapids runs didn't count. We should be happy we avoided a loss, but we're really upset that we didn't win and we were not in a very good mood as we came to Waterloo.

The Waterloo Royals are always tough, they always have excellent prospects and they don't make many mistakes. We were down, 6–2, when thanks to a few Waterloo errors, we rallied to make it 6–5.

Then, in the top of the eighth, Carlos Quinones slices a long drive down the right-field line. The Waterloo right fielder, Ruppert Jones, tried to make a shoestring catch, but missed it and it looked like Quinones would circle the bases for an inside-the-park homer that would tie the score. But the Royals quickly set up their relay and as Carlos rounded third, it was certain a close play would develop at home.

The throw came in and from my vantage point, it looked like Carlos eluded the tag. The umpire didn't think so and he called him out and Carlos went into a rage. When the smoke cleared, Quinones had been thumbed out and suspended for three days for grabbing the umpire and Okrie was ejected for spraying the ump's face with a hot mist of tobacco juice, and we were still losing, 6–5. That's how the game ended.

We got our revenge tonight . . . momentarily, that is. We jumped off to a 4–0 lead, we had to rally for two in the eighth to win, 7–6. It was quite an adventure for Quinones couldn't play and so we put our catcher, Ramon Vega, on first and Slattery caught. Vega responded to his new position with a five RBI night and an errorless game in the field. His three-run homer in the first chased Waterloo starter, Jerry (Lefty) Gomez, and his two-run double in the eighth sealed the victory. It was sweet revenge all the way around, except that Waterloo had the last laugh.

It was a hot, humid night and as we stripped down in the visitors' clubhouse, we were looking forward to a nice, relaxing, invigorating shower.

The shower stalls in the visiting clubhouse in Waterloo are the size of a normal telephone booth and although there are six nozzles on the wall, only two of them were working. To make matters worse, the nozzles are permanently fixed in one position and the water comes spurting out in one thin stream. If you don't play the angle right, even getting wet is difficult.

Consequently Jeff Natchez, my six-foot-three roommate, could only get his legs wet and Steve Vasquez, our diminutive five-foot-seven third baseman, could only get the top of his head wet if he stood on his toes. Waterloo had gotten the better of us with a minor league version of germ warfare.

THOMAS DeFEO

minor league team picture wouldn't be
plete without the bus.

After a brief homestand of two games, we're back on the road again. Here we live in style—early century, that is—at a once fashionable hotel which we've dubbed "Hotel Geriatric."

The temperatures have been in the nineties the last three days with no relief or rain in sight, and our bus rides from Clinton in the heat always knock the stuffing out of you. If you're lucky enough to fall asleep on the bus, you'll be unlucky enough to wake up in a pool of sweat with your throat gagging for something cool to drink. Iowa summers are something else.

I dislike bus rides to begin with, but to make me hate them more I'm sitting there watching town after town pass by, sweating in the hot sun, bathed by the heat outside and the smoke inside. Our team must easily lead the league in one category—cigarettes consumed daily. It seems three-fourths of the team smokes and smokes heavily, so much so that if a bystander saw our bus go by, he'd think the inside was on fire because of the fumes pouring out of the window.

After we've completed our two-and-a-half-hour trek to Burlington, we check into this classic hotel. It must have been the place to stay back in the 1930s, but its quaint charm has begun to wear thin. In fact, its quaint charm is beginning to peel.

There's a choice of rooms, but it's a little complicated. You can have a room with black and white TV and no air conditioning, or a room with air conditioning and no TV, or you can hit the jackpot and get a room with no TV, no air conditioning and no bathroom.

Bill Michael is my roomie on this trip and he was thrilled by our suite. Our air conditioner consists of two propellers hanging from the ceiling, circulating the hot air throughout the room. Billy was really enjoying this bit of nostalgia come true, saying that it reminded him of Humphrey Bogart's bar in "Casablanca" because of the propeller fans.

When we finally got both of them going at full speed, I told Bill if he wanted, we could probably hijack our room back to Clinton. All we had to do was find the cockpit and the pilot.

The one thing in this place that really turns me off is the lobby. It's full of elderly people who have nothing to do but sit around in thick, plush chairs and watch people go by. They don't say anything, not even to each other. They just sit, both men and women, like pieces of furniture waiting patiently until they are replaced.

It was the same when we were here about two months ago. The lobby was full of the same people, just watching and listening to the transients that pass through the hotel.

I have a little bit of social consciousness drilled in me. I don't know exactly where it came from, but I always feel sad in this place. I feel sorry for these people who obviously have no place to go and are literally just waiting for their time to come to an end. It all seems so futile.

But being a ballplayer doesn't allow one to get too caught up in such matters. Baseball is a demanding sport and when one's mind loses its focus on the game and starts drifting away to other worlds, you never play well or enjoy your work.

You just can't play the game of baseball trying to rationalize how you are helping cure the ills of society.

Burlington, Iowa
July 9

It was another of those unbearably hot and humid days and we were scheduled to play an afternoon game. Before the game, as we were getting dressed, all the guys were complaining about the heat until Okrie had enough of such talk.

"The next guy that complains about the heat," Len said, "is getting fined $25. This heat is all in your heads."

179

Just at that minute, Al Newsome came in. He had been out on the field running sprints and he was dripping wet.

"This heat may be all in my head," Al said. "But some of it just dripped from my head to my shirt here."

When the game started, we were up against a crafty control pitcher who was just trying to hit the corners. From the start, the home plate umpire no doubt decided he was going to get this game over with as quickly as possible and that he was going to call everything near the plate a strike, even if Ted Williams couldn't hit it.

I led off and the pitcher threw a lot of low outside pitches and on what I thought was ball four, the umpire said, "Strike Three."

I turned around and before I could say a word, the umpire looked at me and said, "That was a strike, that's the way it is."

I was sort of disgusted, but I figured there was no use arguing, I'd give him that one, but it had better not happen again.

The next batter was Carlos Quinones, back from his three-day suspension. He brought the count to 2–2 and the pitcher came in with the same pitch he had thrown me, low and away, and the umpire called it strike three. Carlos squawked to the umpire, a little more vociferously than I had, but nothing very severe. The umpire apparently was in no mood to listen to any more squawking and he just yelled back at Carlos, who said something back, then walked off the field and threw his bat, cursing a few obscenities over his shoulder, not directly at the umpire, but in the vicinity of home plate.

"Quinones, you're gone," the umpire shouted.

As it turned out, when the smoke had cleared, Carlos had not only been thrown out of a game, but out of a career. Since he was on probation for assaulting an umpire a week earlier, the report went to the league office, where the president of the league decided that Quinones would be suspended for the rest of the season.

When this got back to the front office in Detroit, it was decided that since Carlos was going to be unable to play for the rest of the year, they might just as well release him.

So it turned out that a few words to the umpire, no more than most guys would say in a similar situation, not only cost Carlos Quinones some money, but turned out to be possibly the longest thumbing in the history of professional baseball.

Clinton, Iowa
July 11

We won two games tonight over Quad-Cities, 6–4 and 5–2. Our record is now 10–7 and we're still in first place. I was 2–for–5 for the night with two walks, two runs scored and one RBI.

I also made two errors. One was ridiculous. With two out in the top of the seventh of the first game, we were only one out away from victory. The batter hit a dribbler to second and the ball had a crazy spin on it. Instinctively, I knew I should be wary of this incredibly easy play. I reached down for the ball and it hit my glove and spun away. Error number one.

The next guy walked and the batter was 3–2 when I knew he was going to hit a line shot at me. He did and it was quite a blast. I could do nothing but imitate a hockey goalie and let it smash off my chest, which it did. I quickly scrambled after the ball and flipped it to first, where it glanced off the glove of first baseman Larry Cox. They gave me error number two and I had put us in a hole, in danger of blowing our lead.

Eventually, we got the third out to win the game and between games, in our clubhouse, I grabbed the catcher's chest protector and put it on for a joke. Everybody got a big kick out of it, although it wouldn't have been so funny if we had lost.

The art of manifesting one's frustrations is a science in

181

baseball that takes many forms, none of which should go unnoticed.

Bob Shortell was best known for ripping down the steel door in Anderson whenever he was the losing pitcher, but I remember one time in Charleston when Shorty was particularly frustrated. It was just after a heavy rainfall and the water had formed a deep, two-foot puddle in the dugout. All the players were sitting on top of the dugout because it was too wet to sit inside.

After a particularly frustrating inning on the mound, Shorty came running off the field, feeling that uncontrollable urge to vent his frustrations.

He took his glove and, in sheer anger, flung it into the dugout. Unfortunately, Shorty was so involved in the game he had forgotten the dugout was flooded and it just added to his frustrations to see his glove hit the water with a large splash and slowly sink to the bottom.

Shorty finished the game with another glove while the subs on the team fished for his glove with a couple of coat hangers.

There have been other notable personal explosions. It was also in Charleston that Dan Kaupla, a relief pitcher who hung one too many sliders that particular day, decided to kick the wall in the clubhouse to express his frustrations. What he didn't know was that the clubhouse wall was made of a cheap, thin sheet metal and he was either surprised or satisfied when the entire side of the structure gave way and collapsed.

Ian Fink, another relief pitcher who has been known to become apoplectic at times, once became so infuriated with his performance he literally ripped his glove in half.

Last year over at Quad-Cities, Rich Lawson felt that crazed urge and a poor unfortunate toilet happened to be in his path of frustrated rampage. According to eye witnesses, after Lawson was finished with that toilet only a few pieces of porcelain remained.

I have heard that Al Striano, an outfielder who played last year at Lakeland and a pretty good hitter, had just completed an 0–for–32 streak by bouncing back to the pitcher. Striano was so frustrated that instead of running to first, being called out and then trotting back to the dugout, he just continued to run—he ran past first base, down the right-field line, all the way to the wall. He then circled the warning track, all the way from right field past center and into left and down the left-field line and, finally, back into the dugout.

Now that's frustration!

Clinton, Iowa
July 13

I celebrated my twenty-third birthday in a rare way—I was the hero of a marathon game.

We beat Burlington, 3–2, in fifteen innings when I drove in the winning run with a single.

What was even more amazing was that Gerald Tyler, a lanky, crafty southpaw, pitched the entire game for us, using only 188 pitches and striking out fourteen. A masterful performance.

It was a hot, muggy night, and when the Burlington ace, Carl Sapp, got a two-run lead early in the game on an error, it looked like he would breeze to another victory.

But then with two out and Jackson on second in the seventh, I singled to left to give us a run. I went to second on the throw home from the outfield. The next batter, Bill Michael, slapped an outside fast ball to left and I beat the throw home to tie the score, 2–2. That's how it stayed until the fifteenth.

Meanwhile, each team had numerous chances, but just when it seemed one team would score, the pitching toughened and the defense stiffened and the game went on.

183

In the last of the fifteenth, Burlington finally cracked. Mel Jackson, who runs like a rabbit, sped down the line and beat out an infield hit. Then Tyler, a fine all-around athlete, put down a perfect sacrifice bunt that Burlington's third pitcher of the night threw into right field. That put men on second and third with nobody out and me coming to bat.

I thought I'd be intentionally walked to set up a force at home, but the first pitch came in right over the heart of the plate for strike one. The next pitch was supposed to be a squeeze play, but the pitcher worked from the stretch position and that didn't give Jackson much of a running start. So when the pitch came over the plate, I decided to slug-bunt it somewhere, just to make certain I got the ball down on the ground. To my delight, I hit a sharp line drive in the hole for the game-winning hit.

It was over. Tyler nearly fainted with joy and exhaustion, the crowd, those that had remained through the marathon, gave us a standing ovation and in the locker room, trainer Ken Houston poured a bottle of beer over my head as though we had just won the World Series.

It was a simply idyllic way to celebrate my birthday—I won the game with my bat, had gone 3–for–7 with two RBIs and a walk, scored a run and raised my batting average to .251 . . . and had a beer poured on me, which I must admit, felt pretty good.

Clinton, Iowa
July 16

The man's name is Moe Hill, Elmore Hill to be proper, and he is a living legend, the Hank Aaron of Class A ball.

A tall, thin, but well-muscled black, Moe is rumored to be about twenty-nine years old, a veritable "old man" for a Class A outfielder-first baseman. Moe has the body of a much younger man; he could easily pass for a nineteen-year-old. His skin is very dark and drawn taut over his handsome face and there isn't an ounce of fat on his body.

Moe doesn't say much or show much emotion. Playing for the Wisconsin Rapids Twins, he is their leader, their top hitter and leading RBI man. He's also a good fielder and the word around the league is that when Moe is in the outfield with Gary Ward and Al Woods, nothing falls in but rain.

Moe Hill was largely responsible for the Twins winning the first half of the Northern Division.

Moe is always chewing on a toothpick, both at bat and in the field. He never argues with umpires or makes much noise in the field, but with a bat, he's incredible. He has personally beaten Clinton about four times this year, always getting the big hit at the right time.

Len Okrie simply shakes his head when Moe comes to bat. "Just keep throwing him breaking stuff," Len says, "don't ever throw him that fast ball, boy. I saw Moe back in '72 in Rocky Mount and let me tell ya, he can really pound that ball, son, he can really pound that ball."

Oke will invariably look around for a ballplayer who had played at Rocky Mount and can corroborate his story.

"Hey, Jeffy, you remember ol' Moe Hill back in Rocky Mount, don't ya, son?"

Jeff will be sitting quietly on the bench and he'll nod in agreement.

It is said that Moe can't hit good breaking stuff, but he destroys fast balls. Nobody can throw the ball by him. But Class A pitchers can't throw three breaking balls for strikes and they have to come in with the hard one and that's when Moe cranks up.

So far this year, he's hitting around .330, with twenty-one home runs and sixty RBIs, most of his homers probably coming on fast balls after the pitcher had fallen behind in the count.

Once, while we were up at Appleton, Greg Kuhl was reading the bulletin board at the Appleton ballpark. It had clippings about recent White Sox games. Greg found one that showed Moe Hill had six RBIs and two homers against Appleton in one game, proving Moe destroys other teams as well as ours.

But the interesting part of the article said, "Moe Hill, who wore an Appleton uniform ten years ago. . . ."

The eternal question is why is Moe Hill still in A ball?

And the eternal answer is that nobody knows. All that matters is that when we go to the ballpark to play Wisconsin Rapids tonight, we're going to have to pitch around Moe Hill and not give him any fast balls in game-winning situations if we are to win.

Appleton, Wisc.
July 17

We lost to the Appleton Foxes tonight, 4–3, as the Foxes hit three windblown home runs off our pitcher, Tom Lantz. Down 4–0, we rallied for three runs on singles, errors and walks, but fell short. Lantz, who has a sharp silder that is usually tough on right-handed hitters, hung a few up in the eyes of the Foxes and the balls simply jumped on a jet stream and rode out of the ballpark.

Our team is beginning to develop a pattern. Good solid pitching, tough defense and scratching for runs makes us much like the '69 Mets, exciting to watch and pennant contenders. But we have a very delicate balance. If our pitching breaks down or our defense crumbles, we're lost because we just don't score enough runs. Or if one of our key players gets hurt or is moved up to a higher classification, even that could ruin our pennant chances.

In the first half of the year, the Pilots were a home run hitting team, full of power and lacking speed. We were just like the big league Tigers, raw power, no speed.

Then Gimenez got moved up to AA and Atilano got hurt

Thompson went to Lakeland, Vasquez cooled off and before we knew it, we were like the old Dodgers, scratching for runs.

In our new alignment, I lead off, trying to scratch for a hit or a walk. Bill Michael is second with his good speed and his bunting ability. Al Newsome is third, hitting for average, but beginning to see only breaking balls away, which reduces his ability to hit for power. Then come Vasquez, Vega, Natchez, Jackson and on down the line, an occasional long ball, but generally we have to work for our runs.

The only starting Pilot without good speed now is Ramon Vega, our cherubic catcher. Ramon speaks little English, but he has a likable personality, always laughing and happy. Vega is a fine, intelligent ballplayer and playing with him every day makes you realize what a smart player he is. He knows when to call a pitch-out, how to pitch every batter, when to try a pick-off and, to top this all off, he's technically flawless as a catcher.

Although he doesn't run well, Ramon is hitting .285 and is the best clutch hitter on the team. When he didn't make the All-Star team, he was disappointed, but he kept it within himself. Everybody in Clinton knew Ramon deserved the honor. Even one of the catchers from another team who was chosen on the All-Star squad told me he felt Ramon was the best catcher in the league.

I not only admire Ramon for his playing ability, but for his truly professional attitude. Even more important to me is that although Ramon speaks only a few words of English and never finished high school in Puerto Rico, I never have any problem communicating my ideas, thoughts or feelings to Ramon, and vice versa.

I don't know what will happen to Ramon. He's recognized by Okrie, a former big league catcher himself, as the best defensive catcher in the Detroit organization and a good prospect to be a catcher in the big leagues. But whenever Ramon is asked about his future in baseball, he just laughs

Ramon Vega, our Most Valuable Player, could
be on the way to the majors.

and in pigeon English says, "Me third base . . . softball in beer leagues, go downtown (baseball lingo for home run) every night."

When you lose a game by one run, each player feels his every little mistake could have been the crucial factor. Each error, strikeout, or missed opportunity becomes a painful and personal sore point and can be the cause of a sleepless night.

I got one hit tonight, a triple. It was a good shot, in the gap, and it almost went for a homer. But the joy of hitting a triple was overshadowed by my following at-bat.

It was the top of the eighth and I was leading off. It is my job to get on base, especially when we're losing, 2–1. The Appleton pitcher, Jack Kucek, who has a rising fast ball, started me off with a curve that hung. I swung and fouled it off and cursed myself. I should have hit that pitch out of the park.

The next pitch was another curve, but it broke in the dirt. Then he threw a fast ball that looked like a perfect home run pitch. I swung hard, but the thing took off and I swung under it.

Now the count was 1–2. I stepped out of the batter's box, trying to contemplate the situation, and get all my powers of concentration together.

"Just get a strike and slap it to right," I told myself. "Just slap it to right."

OK. I was ready to go. I crouched a bit more, tucked my shoulder in and got set. A blazing fast ball came in, chest high on the outside corner. I stepped in and swung down on it, trying to slap it. To my amazement the ball rose—like a 747 off a runway—and my carefully planned swing was merely fanning air.

189

It was strike three and I had failed in my mission. I just stood there for a moment, slowly walked back to the bench and sat down.

We lost the game, 2–1, our sixth one-run loss in a row.

It's now 3:30 A.M. I went to bed two and a half hours ago, tossed around, then finally got up. I've seen that same rising fast ball about a hundred times in my mind's eye. I see it coming, coming, and all of a sudden rising away, and I take a vicious swing. I've taken a hundred vicious swings at that fast ball . . .and I haven't hit it yet.

Wisconsin Rapids, Wisc.
July 20

Today is Saturday and every week at about one or two in the afternoon, all minor leaguers around the country gravitate to the television set to get their youthful dreams of baseball recharged. I refer, of course, to the minor leaguer's Shangri-La, the *Major League Game of the Week.*

This is what it's all about, playing in the major leagues. This is why we put up with the long bus rides and the greasy hamburgers, to chase the dream. The *Game of the Week* gets every minor leaguer, whether he is in a slump or doing well, all excited about making it to the golden league some day. You always get a chill down your spine when the starting lineups are announced, pretending it's your name they just said.

Today, the game is something special. The Texas Rangers are playing the Milwaukee Brewers and I have a friend and former opponent playing today on national network TV.

Only one year ago, playing down in Anderson, I'd watch the *Game of the Week,* then go out that evening and do battle with the Gastonia Rangers, led by their hard-hitting first baseman, Mike Hargrove, who was hitting in the neighborhood of .350 or .360 all season.

Mike was a modest, six-foot-one, 200-pounder who offered no clues to his rapid rise to fame. He was the type of

190

amateur player who might have been overlooked as a professional because he never played high school baseball, attended college briefly and was signed on the strength of his showing on the sandlots. He was drafted No. 572.

Mike feasted on our pitching all season. In one two-game series, he went 8–for–9 against us and the only time he went out was when he drilled a line shot right at me and I held on to it. As I came into the dugout and passed Mike, who was going to first base, I kidded him.

"Don't let it get you down, Mike, just hang in there."

Now Mike is playing in the big leagues. He made the big jump in just one year, which is phenomenal. Even more phenomenal, he not only made the big jump, the season is half over and he's hitting over .350 and is among the batting leaders in the American League.

It's incredible and it couldn't have happened to a nicer guy.

A year ago, he was hitting about the same in the Class A Western Carolinas League and although he was well-respected throughout our league, nobody expected anything like this. At best, they thought Mike might have jumped to AA or AAA. Usually, a good year in Gastonia will get you promoted, but not too high. He's done the impossible, jumping from Class A to the bigs in one year.

When Mike came to bat for the first time, Curt Gowdy mentioned that he had hit .351 in the Western Carolinas League last year. He added that the second-leading hitter batted only .290. It made me feel pretty good about my .246.

In today's game, Mike went 3–for–4. Jim Colborn of the Brewers tried to pitch him low and inside, but I could have told him his strategy wouldn't work. We tried to pitch him low and inside last year when he got those eight hits in a doubleheader.

Most of the guys I played with or against last year I can follow in the back pages of *The Sporting News,* in the minor league section.

I have some interest in Claudell Washington, the Oakland A's sensational rookie, because he played in the Midwest League last year with Burlington. But I didn't play against him. Most of the guys I played against last year are in Pittsfield or Thetford Mines or St. Petersburg. Only one went from the Western Carolinas League to the big leagues—Mike Hargrove.

Wausau, Wisc.
July 21

On the fourth day of a five-day road trip, we headed up to a place approximately 200 miles north of Milwaukee, which seemed like twenty miles south of the North Pole. I expected to see Santa's reindeer and his elves at any minute.

We were going to play the Wisconsin Rapids Twins on a field here in Wausau, a regular league game but at a new site, possibly a future league city.

We climbed on the bus at our motel and forty-five minutes later, after traveling through the hills and woods of western Wisconsin, we pulled into this quaint little town which was obviously a resort area.

Lloyd, our bus driver, stopped the first few people he saw in town and asked where the ballpark was. It was very distressing because the first three people he stopped didn't know and the town couldn't have been that big.

Eventually, we found it and the ballpark was an old, old structure that looked like a fortress. It was made of stone and had barbed wire fences all around the place.

We went inside and our worst fears came true. First, the entire seating area was enclosed by this wire mesh fence, so that it was almost impossible for anybody to look in or out. It was a very strange phenomenon because when people came into the ballpark, it looked like they were just painted faces up in the stands.

We soon noticed that the sun was going to set right behind center field in a direct line with the pitcher and that

192

makes hitting very difficult when you can't see the ball. We couldn't even see the pitcher.

The Twins' pitcher was a slow, control pitcher who never got more than three strikeouts a game, but he looked like Sandy Koufax to us in the first three innings because nobody could see the ball.

I think the pitcher soon became aware that we were having trouble seeing him. Newsome tipped him off by wearing his sunglasses to the plate.

When I went to bat, the sun behind him was so brilliant you just couldn't see anything. I'm convinced that on the second strike, he just went through the motions of winding up, pretending to throw and the catcher slapped his glove.

The umpire called strike two and I turned to him and asked ever so politely, "Did you see where that pitch went?"

"No, not really," he confessed.

"Then, why did you call it a strike?"

"I don't know," he replied. "I just figured the ball was blocked out by the sun, so it must have been in the strike zone."

How are you going to argue with that logic?

Clinton, Iowa
July 22

Today is the All-Star break and it couldn't come soon enough. As of today, the Clinton Pilots, once the scourge of our division in this second half, are now 13–14, and are in third place in the division. Just five days ago, as we left for our last road trip to Appleton and Wisconsin Rapids, we were 13–9 and in first place. In other words, we have just lost five in a row.

It's a six-and-a-half-hour bus ride from Wisconsin Rapids back to Clinton. Think about it, six and a half hours on a hot, steamy, smoky bus with a team that has just lost five in a row and dropped out of first place. It's not a very pleasant experience, believe me.

The first few hours were fairly quiet, most of the guys cramping their bodies into the small seats and trying to sleep in the hot summer air. Occasionally, someone blurts out a curse word when the realization sets in that we have just blown our first-place lead, or when someone gets a muscle spasm that occurs easily, and often, on so long a ride.

About two hours later—mind you, we still have four and a half hours left—the silence was broken by a singular, sarcastic voice from the back of the bus. Tom Lantz, a veteran of many bus rides from Wisconsin Rapids to Clinton (he played at Clinton last year, too) screams in masochistic delight: "Oh, my God, four and a half hours to go. Somebody put me in a straightjacket. I'm not going to make it this time. Somebody get me a straightjacket before I go crazy."

Unlike the shorter bus rides in Anderson, which seemed to have a touch of good fellowship even if we lost five in a row, this year's bus rides tend to be a bit more caustic, humorous, but with a bite in them. Laughter is frequent, but it is usually sadistic.

After Lantz' pleas, which act as the opening statement in the bus rides' affairs, everybody begins to awaken from their nap. The Puerto Ricans begin to chatter loudly, jabbering in their native tongue, and all the guys who smoke instinctively light up their cigarettes. Soon the bus is wide awake again and the mischief of a frustrated ball team is about to commence.

Bill Michael, the number one mischief maker who resembles an impish little elf with a Brillo pad for hair, will get the ball rolling. Noticing that the bus is headed for a stretch of road that is under construction, he senses a new game to play.

On the roadside are a whole line of flashing lights, propped up on wooden horses in order to keep traffic in a

194

straight line. Bill grabs a broom from the top of the luggage rack and, opening one of the windows, pokes the wooden broom out and attempts to knock off the yellow flashing lights.

This game is only partially successful as only a few yellow lights are hit. It gets a few big laughs, but the laughter soon dies down.

Meanwhile, in the back of the bus, Lantz yells out, "Gimme the electric chair, anything but this bus."

But Michael sees another opportunity. Grabbing a pitcher of water, and seeing that Rich Lawson has momentarily vacated his seat, Michael quickly inundates Lawson's seat with the water. A few seconds later, Lawson returns innocently to his place, sits down and thoroughly soaks his pants, much to the delight of all the guys.

Seeking revenge, Lawson grabs the pitcher and douses Michael over the head with the remaining water. More sadistic laughter.

The laughter subsides and somebody mentions that we're only three hours from home. From the back, Lantz shouts, "Anybody got an extra pair of handcuffs I could borrow?"

Michael has had enough. He's tired and he decides to try to sleep. But his seat is wet because Lawson took over his seat and left Bill with the wet one. Billy quickly jumps on top of the seats and raises himself up onto the luggage rack overhead. There he hoists up a pillow and lies in the luggage rack, comfortably tucked away as if he were in a hay loft. There he would stay for the remainder of the trip.

Meanwhile in the back, Lantz is still going slowly insane. Then, in the middle of the night, Lantz awakens everybody in the bus again.

"Look," he shouts. "Look, there it is. We're home. There it is."

Sure enough, there's the giant Planters Peanuts silo rising well above the town of Clinton, and there he is with his top hat and monocle, good old Mr. Peanut.

"Sweet are the uses of adversity," wrote William Shakespeare.

Ol' country boy, Al Newsome, whose words are punctuated by a bobbing toothpick in the side of his mouth, told me before the game with Waterloo that his recent illness made him a better hitter.

The Georgia strong man had been pounding the ball at a .350 clip when he developed a bad cold, which spread to his ears. They became so clogged, he couldn't hear. As his average tumbled game by game, Al said with his sense of hearing gone, it was imperative that he compensate by complete concentration on watching the ball. Now that his hearing has come back, his concentration has remained.

Noose had four more hits tonight, his second four-hit night in a row, and his average zoomed to .371.

I had a pretty good night myself, two doubles and a single, as we beat Waterloo for the second straight night. I also got some good-natured kidding from Mickey Vernon, the former great major leaguer who is now the Royals' organizational batting coach. Vernon knew my dad when they were both working in Washington and he remembers me when I was just a little shaver.

After the game, Newsome told me his thinking at the plate has changed.

"Now I think fast ball," he confided, "and adjust to the curve. Before I was trying to get set for the curve when I felt it might be coming and they'd breeze the fast one right by me."

I used to get a big kick out of reading a *Sporting News* publication, "Knotty Problems of Baseball." We had one of our own tonight that was never covered in the booklet.

THOMAS DeFEO

' country boy Al Newsome is one of the
aracters I'll never forget.

We were leading Appleton, 4–3, in the ninth when Mike Wolf, their batter, hit a pop up with one out. Our shortstop Mel Jackson moved under it and waited for it to come down. When it did, the ball came down with a bird. It seems the ball had hit a large nighthawk circling overhead and when they both came down, Mel wisely ignored the bird and caught the ball.

After we had won the game, Len Okrie heaved a sigh of relief.

"I didn't want any foul-up on that call," he cracked.

As for Mel Jackson, he said he simply figured a "ball in the hand . . ."

Dubuque, Iowa
July 29

This was a big night for my old roommate and teammate from Anderson, George Cappuzzello. After his excellent pitching last year, Cappy was assigned to Lakeland. But when he wasn't pitching much, they assigned him to the Dubuque Packers in our league.

Dubuque is not affiliated with any specific major league team. It is a cooperative team, meaning it draws its players from several organizations. Cappy, of course, is still the property of Detroit while he is in Dubuque.

When we arrived here, we were in the middle of the race for the second-half championship and quite concerned with our chances. Every game was a big one and we wanted to sweep the Packers if we could.

It turned out to be an unusual night. When we arrived at the ballpark, we had no idea Cappuzzello was scheduled to pitch against us. We hadn't seen him in quite some time and we chatted and kidded with him before the game. It was good seeing him again.

He seemed very loose, although there was a tremendous

198

amount of pressure on the kid. He wanted to do well against the team from his parent organization; he wanted to show us that he could still do the job. He knew Okrie would be sending in a report after the game and he wanted that report in the home office to be favorable toward him.

To make things even more dramatic, Cappy's parents had come all the way from Ohio for a few days and when you're a pitcher and your parents come to see you for a few days, everything is focused on one game. You pretty much have only one chance to make good for them, not like an everyday player who can have a bad game and still make it up the next night. When Cappy pitched again, his mom and dad would most likely be gone.

So the stage was set for the big battle and I was a little worried about facing Cappy because I knew him from last year. He was my roomie and I came to know him as a good pitcher and a tough competitor and I was concerned as to how I might do against him.

As much as I wanted him to do a good job because I thought he needed a break, I was more concerned with myself and my team and how we would do against him. I wanted to hit him, get at least two hits off him and hit the ball solidly.

As it turned out, he pitched a brilliant game, using his fast ball, slider, curve and an excellent strikeout pitch, a side arm change-up, very well.

I walked in my first time at bat when he missed the low inside corner with a 3–1 fast ball. I also lined out to center and lined out to right.

It was a tough 2–1 loss for us and it hurt our pennant chances. Naturally, we were all disappointed after losing such a tough game, but at the same time, I felt a lot of the guys had a kind of inner happiness that George had done such an excellent job because when Oke makes his report, he's certain to give Cappy a good word and maybe they will give him a break for next year.

One of the highlights of every day from spring training through the end of the season is receiving mail. The letters are like base hits, you savor every one, craving news from home.

Some days you get shut out and that only makes you look forward all the more to tomorrow.

A road trip always seems shorter when you start out with a letter to read and reread on the bus. It stirs up thoughts of home and friends and, for a while, your mind relaxes and takes you away from the tedious, everyday world of baseball.

There was a letter waiting for me today. It was from the president of the Midwest League. He was officially acknowledging one of my baseball firsts. I was fined $10 for arguing a call in the game against Appleton ten days ago.

One of the big attractions of professional ball, at least to me, is the camaraderie and respect that develops among players not only on your own team, but on opposing teams, as well. This is the essence of sports.

By the middle of the season, you've gotten to know the players on other teams as individuals, not just as men in uniforms.

You have so much in common, starting with the will to make good and get up to the big leagues. It's easy to appreciate each other's successes and failures because you have successes and failures of your own. You play against the same people over and over, read about them and you often share funny stories with them before a game.

Everybody knows how difficult it is to succeed and that, I suppose, is the common denominator among all players. An outstanding play or a good solid performance is admired, even if it's at your expense.

Midwest League of Professional Baseball Clubs, Inc.

OUR MEMBER CITIES' MOST VALUABLE SPORTS ASSET

POST OFFICE BOX 444   BURLINGTON, IOWA 52601

August 5, 1974

Mr. Rick Wolfe
Clinton Baseball Club
P. O. Box 789
Clinton, Iowa 52732

Dear Mr. Wolfe,

I have reviewed the umpire's report of the Midwest League game at Clinton on July 27th.

The report states that you were ejected for prolonged arguing of a called third strike in accordance with Rule 90₂A, and that you also showed your dissatifaction with the call by kicking dirt on home plate.

For this you are fined $10.00 payable to this office five days from your receipt of this letter.

Sincerely,

William K. Walters

WKW/e

William K. Walters
President

WM. K. WALTERS, PRESIDENT
POST OFFICE BOX 444
BURLINGTON, IOWA 52601
319/752-5345
752-2444

GEO. CLIFFORD, VICE PRESIDENT
1631 PARK TOWNE CT. N.E.
CEDAR RAPIDS, IOWA 52402

DORIS KRUCKER, SECRETARY
629 BROWN ST., APT. 1
DAVENPORT, IOWA 52802

A couple of days ago I hit a line shot to left against Dubuque. The packer left fielder, Joe Rubertino, raced back to the wall, leaped up and caught the ball with one hand as he smashed into the fence.

A sure double had been turned into another out. I'm no better sport than anybody else and the way I've been going I need all the hits I can get, but it was a tremendous play by Rubertino and when I passed him on the field at the end of the inning, I told him so and he thanked me. That was the entire conversation.

A few weeks ago we were in Appleton playing the White Sox. Their pitcher was throwing a great game. He fired bee-bees as he struck out thirteen and I was his victim three times, as he sawed off our bats with a blazing, rising fast ball. But I did manage to make contact once and I laced a solid triple off the right-center field wall.

As I was dusting myself off on third, the pitcher, who had gone over to back up the play, walked by me on his way back to the mound and said, "Good hit, Rick."

"Thanks," I said, "they're tough to come by against you."

I meant what I said because he could really fire the ball.

The reason I mention all this is because I picked up the Chicago *Tribune* today and read that the White Sox had just called up that Appleton pitcher, Jack Kucek.

Imagine, two weeks ago I was facing him in the Class A Midwest League, and today Jack Kucek is in the majors. It's staggering.

Danville, Ill.
August 8

History was made today. The President of the United States re-signed from office.

It's sad to say that most of the players on the Clinton and Danville teams that met in tonight's game, were more concerned with their batting averages, their earned-run averages or where they were going to eat after the game.

I don't think it's that they weren't interested, but that's what happens when you play minor league baseball and you are so involved in your own life and death struggle to make good. You have a tendency to become unconcerned with anything that happens in the world outside.

Some of us were interested in today's development, however, Greg Kuhl in particular. Greg is a very aware young man. His father is a newspaperman in Montgomery, Alabama, and Greg is a trivia nut specializing in two subjects—colleges and Watergate. As the team's resident expert on the Watergate proceedings, he knows everything there is to know about it. Sometimes it seems he knows more about it than President Nixon or his lawyers.

We knew the President was going to address the nation tonight and Greg had a hunch it meant resignation, so he took a portable radio with him to the ballpark and had it in the bullpen.

Radios in the bullpen are not uncommon. In fact, Jack Walsh, one of our pitchers last year, had a little game he would play when he got bored down there. He'd have the ballgame on and things were going along quietly and all of a sudden Jack would get up and start limbering up, even though he hadn't gotten a sign from Len to do so. The reason he did it, Jack said, is because he wanted to hear the announcer say, "There's action in the Clinton bullpen . . . Let's see, that's Jack Walsh starting to throw." Then once he'd heard his name, Jack would sit down and listen for the announcer to say, "Now Walsh has stopped throwing."

I was rather upset to think about what was going on and here I was playing baseball. In Washington, a man is making a speech that will affect 250 million Americans, the whole world, in fact, and here I am in Middle America playing a minor league baseball game and, what's more, there are 400 people in the stands watching the game.

THOMAS DeF

The boys in the bullpen.

There was no announcement over the PA when the President finished speaking. But Kuhl walked into the dugout from the bullpen and I knew that meant the speech was over.

"Did he resign?" I asked, and Greg just nodded, and that was all.

Later, when the game was over, you couldn't even get most of the guys to talk about it. If you were to mention to most of them that President Nixon resigned, they would probably say, "That's fine. Where do we eat?"

Danville, Ill.
August 9

There are not many original things that can be done during the playing of the national anthem, but tonight I witnessed a new twist, which was interesting in light of recent events.

There wasn't a big crowd on hand for the game and so when the public address announcer asked the fans to rise for the playing of the national anthem, it was easy to see—and hear—who was doing the singing.

To my amazement, the loudest voices came from the Danville dugout. There were the Danville non-starters, all lined up as pert as choir boys with their caps off and over their hearts. What's more, they were lined up according to height, the tallest guys at one end and the smallest ones at the other end.

To cap it off, Danville manager Matt Galante, a diminutive, Napoleonic five-foot-seven ex-infielder, was at the very end of the line, the smallest guy there, and leading his troops in harmony much in the manner of Arthur Fiedler leading the Boston Pops.

The anthem continued, the Danville players gleefully singing, filling the park with the lyrics of Francis Scott Key's famous song. They weren't exactly the Mormon Tabernacle Choir, but all things considered, it was a very impressive showing.

THOMAS DeF[

It's an old baseball custom, even in the minors . . .
I'm left of the dugout post.

THOMAS DeFEO

Before tonight's game, Len Okrie called Eddie Morrison into his office and Eddie's heart sank. Whenever the manager wants to see you, you always think the worst—you've been released or there's trouble back home.

That was not the case this time. Okrie had received a telephone call from Detroit. It was Ralph Houk, the Tiger manager. They were playing the Rangers and Mike Hargrove was wearing them out.

Somehow, Houk got word that Morrison had handled Hargrove pretty well in Anderson last year. In one particular game, Eddie struck Hargrove out twice, so Houk was calling to find out how Morrison had pitched him.

Okrie called Eddie in and put him on the telephone with the Major. It was Morrison's big moment. At least he knew the Tiger manager knew of his existence, which is more than most of us could say.

Hoot Evers, the main boss, is in town for his usual visit and whenever he shows up, all sorts of weird things happen. Because of the pressure of playing in front of the "man that counts" in the Detroit organization, ballplayers are liable to perform in some atypical ways—good base runners will get picked off, good hitters will suddenly and inexplicably go into slumps, weak hitters look like Ty Cobb, good fielders make errors on the easiest plays and ordinary fielders make circus catches.

The only true way of evaluating a player is over a long stretch of time, preferably over an entire season.

Because I had the experience of playing in front of Hoot,

I wasn't intimidated this time. I was determined to just play my usual brand of ball regardless of who was watching me.

Much to my amazement I played pretty well while Hoot was here for his short visit. I made all the plays in the field and was getting some important hits.

But tonight was a bittersweet performance. We were playing the Cedar Rapids Astros and it was a 1–1 standoff until the bottom of the twelfth when I drove in the winning run with my first hit of the night. I was 1–for–6 on the evening.

I thought that it showed a lot of guts and that Hoot would be especially pleased with my effort. Earlier in the game I had been doing badly. I bunted into a force play, popped up, struck out. But with the bases loaded in the bottom of the twelfth, I lined the first pitch to right to win the game. I got the big hit when it counted most.

I was feeling pretty good and since this was the last Clinton game Hoot would see this year, I figured he'd come down into the locker room as he usually does and give everybody (me especially) a well-deserved pat on the back.

But Hoot never showed up in the locker room. Because the game was so long, he had to leave in the ninth inning to catch his plane back to Detroit and he never did see my game-winning hit.

Waterloo, Iowa
August 15

I think the word is out around the league that I'm writing a book about my minor league experiences. The reason I say that is today Harold Thomasson, the third baseman for the Waterloo Royals, hit a drive to left and hustled around first and headed for second.

Newsome picked up the ball and fired it into me and Thomasson slid in with a cloud of dust, just ahead of my tag.

After the umpire called him safe, Thomasson looked up at me and said, "Hey, Rick, will this make the book?"

Suppose Harold had tripled, I wondered. Would he have dropped me a note as he rounded second?

Cedar Rapids, Iowa
August 19

The fellows were talking about Tom Underwood, an excellent pitcher who suffered through a nightmare on coast-to-coast television tonight. Tom made his major league debut on the *Monday Night Game of the Week,* pitching for the Philadelphia Phillies against the Cincinnati Reds. He struck out his first man, then was rapped for six hits in a row before leaving for shelter.

It brought back memories to all the Anderson Survivors of the night when Al Newsome blasted three home runs and a double against Spartanburg last year. Tom Underwood started that game, too.

But Tom also pitched a lot of good games to warrant being called up to the bigs. It seems there are good days and bad days in the majors, just like in the minors. It's all part of baseball's inevitable balancing process. The only difference is if you have a bad day in the majors, you're already there, but enough bad days in the minors and you may never get there.

Clinton, Iowa
August 21

I've been thinking back over the season and it just dawned on me that I've played in every game, every inning, since the night after graduation, way back in June. That includes doubleheaders, seven games a week, with no time and a half for overtime.

I prefer it that way. Of course, the little bumps and bruises begin to take their toll because you don't have a chance to get rid of them. I have a bruised right ankle, a sprained left thumb, a sore left elbow, numerous strawberries from sliding, scraped knees and a few more things that have slipped my mind momentarily.

Last year there was more healing time when I platooned with Nat Calamis, but this season I've had the opportunity to stay in the lineup as the other second basemen dropped off. I've really enjoyed the regular work. Playing every day keeps you sharp and gives you a better feel of the game and of your performances.

It's tiring, but stamina is part of the game, too. Len Okrie knows when we're bushed or aching and it means that much more to him when you're still able to play and do well.

One thing this regular play has done is give me a lot more respect for one record I never really gave too much thought to before. I mean Lou Gehrig's record of playing in 2,130 consecutive games. Let's see, only about 2,086 to catch him.

Clinton, Iowa
August 22

Al Newsome's late-season batting slump has cost him a chance at the league batting title. Old Moe Hill of Wisconsin Rapids has it all but wrapped up now.

While Noose slumped, Ol' Moe, just like Ol' Man River, kept right on rolling along. It is now a certainty that Moe will lead the league in hits, home runs, RBIs, total bases and batting average.

After the kind of year he had this year, it will be interesting to see if Moe will still be playing in Class A next year.

211

I picked up a copy of *The Sporting News* today and read both good and bad news. Unfortunately, the good news is not good enough to wipe away the bad.

The good news is that Miguel Dilone, the talented Charleston base stealer who got the ceremonial base by breaking the Western Carolinas base-stealing record last year against Anderson, has been called up to the Pittsburgh Pirates. Dilone had over 100 stolen bases this year at Salem in the Carolina League and was called up, proving once again that the Impossible Dream is really not impossible.

The bad news is that one of Dilone's teammates, an eighteen-year-old kid named Alfredo Edmead, was killed in a freak accident after a collision going after a pop fly.

I didn't know Edmead, but I do know Dilone, who was his friend and countryman, both players coming from the Dominican Republic. You don't have to know someone to mourn his death. He was, after all, another human being and another minor league ballplayer.

Just two more runs, that's all we needed to stay in the pennant race.

As of three days ago, the Clinton Pilots, to the surprise of all, were only a game and a half behind division-leading Danville. What's more, we had to play a three-game series in Burlington and the Bees were only two games behind Danville.

With the season ending in just a few days, winning those three games against Burlington was essential if we were to keep our hopes alive. And, of course, Burlington felt that they still had a chance at the title, too. So the entire season boiled down into one three-game series and you could feel the pressure mounting.

In the first game, I felt we outplayed and outhustled the Bees, an affiliate of the Oakland A's, but somehow we lost in the thirteenth inning by a score of 4–3.

All I can recall about the game is that the key blow for the Bees was delivered by a young third baseman named Hooper, who was hitting only .054 at the time of his hit. It was the kind of defeat that leaves you shaking your head in disgust, but also with a desire for revenge.

And that's how we felt after the second game. We figured we had been cheated out of victory the night before (we still couldn't get over being beaten by an .054 hitter) and we were out to take this second game of the series. This was the crucial game. We had to win this one.

We had our ace southpaw, Elliott Moore, who had been returned from Montgomery to help us in our pennant drive, going for us, and the Michigan State graduate curved and finessed his way into the ninth inning. We were playing good tough baseball behind him and as the Bees came up for their last at-bat in the bottom of the ninth, the 1–0 lead looked safe. Just three more outs and the tide will be turned in our favor.

But what's that about the game never being over until the last out? Now we know all about it.

Matt Keough, son of former major leaguer Marty Keough, was called on to pinch-hit. Matt is a fine shortstop, but he's a slap hitter and not considered a long ball threat. I'm sure he was just looking to get on base any way he could and I guess Elliott was thinking the same thing and determined not to walk the tying run to first. So, when the count went to 3–2, Elliott just wanted to throw a strike and he poured in a high fast ball.

Keough jumped on the pitch and to the amazement of all, lofted it over the left field wall to tie the score. The Pilots were stunned, but we kept enough of our poise to get the next two batters out.

We had to get one more out to send the game into extra innings, but Mark Budaska singled to keep the game going and, before we knew what happened, Gary Woods lined a shot that hit right on the left-field line. Budaska, running on the crack of the bat, came all the way around to score and we were beaten, 2–1.

Our dressing room was like a morgue after the game, with Elliott Moore suffering more than any of us. He had pitched a masterful game, but he had lost our biggest game of the year.

The next day was hot and muggy and in the Iowa heat and humidity we had an afternoon game. We struggled valiantly, only to lose, 4–2. We had lost all three games to Burlington, our pennant hopes were crushed. All you heard on the ride home was the whirr of tires.

Now, we're back in Clinton again, the disastrous road trip ended, our pennant chances dashed away by a total of four runs in three games. I don't know why it is, but in baseball the wins just sort of blur together and the losses stand out . . . especially those sharp, painful losses when a pennant is at stake and you lose in the late innings.

Those are the kind that keep you awake at night . . . and when you're in the minor leagues, you can't even say, "Wait 'til next year."

Clinton, Iowa
August 29

Tonight is the last game of the season and it is our big give-away night, designated by Pilot General Manager, Fritz Colschen, as "Broken Bat Night." Every child who attends the game in the company of an adult, gets an official, authentic, authorized Clinton Pilot broken bat.

The promotion is just like the big league's bat day give-aways, except that ours are broken, personally smashed and cracked by the members of the Clinton Pilots throughout the season with the help of fist-jamming fast balls thrown by opposing pitchers and saved all season for this special occasion.

I didn't think the idea behind "Broken Bat Night" was too bad. Now all we need to have is a "Free Tape and Nails Night" so that the kids will be able to fix their broken bats.

Come to think of it, I imagine Fritz has already thought of that.

Brighton, Mass.
September 15

Once more, I've exchanged my baseball flannels for academic robes and I'm a "rookie" again—a rookie in law school, that is.

After the final game of the season, I caught a ride from Clinton early the next morning and took a noon plane out of Chicago's O'Hare Field. I had a few days at home before it was time to become a student once again.

I'm settled in now, having completely made the transition from jock to student. I have my own apartment, a pile of books and plenty of work.

It's hard to believe that just a few weeks ago I completed my second full year of professional baseball. Two full years. It sure doesn't seem that long. In fact, I can still remember sitting on an airplane, writing a letter home, eager and nervous as any raw rookie would be as I headed for Florida and my first spring training.

The inevitable question then was, "Am I good enough to make it?"

Today I would be known in the Class A circuit as a hardened veteran and that question has been partially answered in both the affirmative and the negative. However, that original question has been altered somewhat. Now I ask, "Will I be asked back next season?"

I really don't know the answer at this point. I felt I improved quite a bit this past season. My hitting was stronger in every department except batting average and that I attribute to my slow start, 19 for 100 at the beginning of the season.

215

Still, even after that bad start I finished at .232, with 13 doubles, 5 triples, 1 home run, 45 runs scored and 16 stolen bases.

I think I'll be asked back, but if not, then I could have played my last professional game. Forever.

It makes me sad to contemplate that. It is conceivable that I'll never wear the uniform of a professional baseball team again, I'll never again hear my name announced in a starting lineup, never again stand at second base with my hat off as the national anthem is played.

It is a very sobering thought, one that I keep trying to banish from my mind. Just in case, let the record show that in my last game, I was 2–for–4, including a base hit on my very last at-bat.

It was kind of funny, too, because on my third time at bat, I looked at a called strike three. So when I came to bat the next time, I knew this was going to be my last at-bat of the season and, after working the count to 1–2 against All-Star pitcher Dave Garcia, I hit his next pitch, a fast ball, for a clean line drive single to center field.

And now that I think about it, that may have been the last hit of my career, a pleasant way to end a career.

As I immerse myself in a new world, a world of torts and contracts and whereases, I'll keep checking the mail every day until I learn whether or not the Tigers want me to continue my baseball career.